Nothing Hidden

Deborah Edmisten

*For Daddy~
Thank you for becoming my daddy ~
I'm so very grateful for the man you are*

.

CHAPTER ONE
Spring 2006

Ashleigh Craig stared at the shaking hands she held in her own, studying the serpentine veins that ran beneath the translucent peaks of wrinkled skin. She felt Mona begin to tremble as the silence grew longer. Ashleigh squeezed the aged fingers reassuringly, fighting the urge to cry. She knew Mona was begging her to believe what most people would discount as the senile ramblings of an elderly woman on the brink of death.

"You're my last hope!" Mona said forcefully as she fought for the breath to articulate her plea. "All my life, I've been afraid to search for an answer, but now I *need* to know. If you won't help me, I'll go to my grave a haunted woman. I can't do it myself. My body is a prison, and this nursing home is my warden."

She paused, delving deeper into her reserves of strength in order to go on. "Be my arms and legs and help me find answers. I know my days are numbered. Until you experience it, there's no way you could possibly understand this feeling. It's as if there's a center to me, and my life is slowly draining from that center and ebbing away. There isn't much time, Ashleigh. A couple of months, maybe. Please, let me tell you my story. Help me to die in peace."

Ashleigh looked up, her dark brown eyes locking with the force of Mona's gaze. The resolve in Mona's eyes confirmed to Ashleigh that her story wouldn't be the incoherent wanderings of an old woman's decaying mind, but that her words would be fact. Even as the feeble body wasted away, the mind of this woman before her was still pulsing with a vibrancy that refused to be quenched. The strength of Mona's determination seemed to meld itself into Ashleigh's soul as the two women – one young, one old – connected in a moment of solidarity more powerful than the odds against them.

"Alright," Ashleigh said, making up her mind. "Start from the very beginning and tell me the whole story. Take your time."

She became completely engrossed as Mona's eyes grew misty and her voice dropped almost to a whisper. As the story unfolded, Ashleigh felt herself being tangibly carried away to a place where the events of eighty years ago were more real than the small, knick-knack cluttered room she sat in.

"It had been a dismally rainy day. One of those lazy days where you lounge around the house reading a book. Mother had gone to visit a friend for the day, and only Father, Peter and myself were at home. Peter was a year old at the time. I was seven. I still remember each moment of that day as if it were yesterday. It was September 5, 1926. Father had cracked the windows slightly to let in the fresh scent of the rain. He loved the smell of the rain. I was sitting on the floor by the fireplace playing with my dolls. Peter was napping. Every so often I would look up at the gently blowing curtains.'

"Even now, I remember feeling that they seemed like hands reaching out as they blew in the wind. As if they were trying to warn me of some imminent danger. My dolls suddenly seemed to be staring at me in wide-eyed fear. Without knowing why, I had a horrible seven-year-old sense of foreboding. I recall it so clearly, Ashleigh, and in the next minutes, my life would be forever changed from the blissfully happy existence it had been up until that time. I watched Father as he sat in his chair reading. He looked up and smiled warmly...the last smile I would ever receive from him. Then there was a knock at the front door. From my spot on the floor, I watched Father get up and walk over to see who it was. I can still picture him carefully pulling aside the lace curtains on the window to see who was knocking."

Tears began to stream down Mona's pale, wrinkled face as she paused, the vision of the past filling and overpowering her senses. "Father's face instantly took on an expression I'd never seen before. One of absolute fear…and something like hatred at the same time. He seemed paralyzed as the knocking continued. He backed away from the window very slowly. When he turned to me, his face was stricken. As if he was a man who had just stared into the face of evil itself. He ran over and grabbed me off the floor and carried me up the steps to my bedroom upstairs. As he sat me down, I tried to ask him what was happening and why he was so afraid…but he put his hand over my mouth to quiet me. He was bristling with panic. It was like my body was signaling an internal warning...I stood frozen in place beside him without making a sound.'

"In total silence, we listened to the crazed banging on the front door. Father paced back and forth like a caged animal, breathing heavily. And then Peter began to cry. As Peter cried, I heard a woman on the front porch start screaming in an enraged voice. I could hear every word because my bedroom window faced the front porch, and it was open slightly. She said, 'I know you're in there, Richard! Open this door, or you'll regret it for the rest of your life! Open this door, *now!*'

"Father bent down, staring into my eyes with a fear that haunts me to this day. 'Mona, I'm going to close your bedroom door when I go out. Whatever you do, don't open it! You must be completely still! Don't make a sound! Do you understand me? You must *not* open the door!' I nodded but didn't say a word. I was so confused. He put his finger over his lips, signaling me to be quiet as he backed out of the room, closing the door behind him. I'll never forget the terror in his eyes. They begged me to obey as if our very lives depended on it. I heard him rush down the stairs, and the creak of the front door as it opened.'

"From that moment on, my thoughts became a whirl of bewilderment as I tried to make sense of the words the woman was yelling. 'How dare you! How dare you think you could do that to me! Didn't you think I would find you?' I heard father pleading with her to calm down. To be rational.'

"In the next instant, I heard the sound of footsteps running up the stairs and Father screaming in horror. 'No, Eunice! You can't do this! *Stop!*' Every second seemed to tick by in slow motion. My bedroom door suddenly seemed larger than life. I walked toward it and put my hand on the doorknob. I was so afraid for Father! I didn't know what was happening. I could hear Peter screaming inconsolably. The yelling between Father and the woman grew louder.'

"My mind was so consumed by fear, I couldn't even comprehend what they were saying. My hand seemed to have a will of its own as I very slowly turned the doorknob, opening the door ever-so-slightly. As I looked out through the small gap, I saw Father and the woman struggling violently at the top of the steps. Her hair was wild, and her eyes were full of pure hatred. She clawed at Father's face as he tried to restrain her. I opened the door all the way when I heard Father moan as if he was in terrible pain. Every protective instinct in my body cried out for action! I shouted at the woman to leave him alone. She instantly stopped attacking Father and stared at me with a look of shock and disbelief. She seemed so familiar, and yet I was certain I'd never seen her before. Then she began to laugh…a wicked, horrible cackle. She looked directly at Father and threw back her head, closing her eyes and roaring with laughter.'

"Father's eyes darted to me then back to the woman…and then…his face…*transformed*. His eyes narrowed to slits, and he reached out and grabbed the woman and shoved her down the steps with all his strength. I don't know if I'll ever forget her scream and the sickening thud of her body as it careened down the steps…and the deadly silence afterward. As stillness filled the air, Father's expression drastically changed again. He held out his hands and looked at them in horror…then he fell to the floor sobbing.'

"I ran to him and embraced his trembling body. I could see the woman at the bottom of the steps with her dark black hair covering her face. I remember the rain beating against the hall windows and thunder rolling in the distance as Father grabbed me by the shoulders and shook me ferociously. 'Why didn't you listen? Look what you've done! *Why didn't you listen?'* He shoved me away and then looked around in desperation, cringing as he glanced down at the woman's body lying on the floor at the bottom of the stairs. A terrible remorse engulfed me as I slowly inched away from him."

Mona paused, a far-away look filling her eyes. "And then something incredible happened. I thought the woman was dead, but she began to moan! Father's head jerked toward the sound as the realization that she wasn't dead seemed to dawn on him. He grabbed me roughly and rushed me into Peter's room. 'Stay here with Peter! Calm him down. Play with him. Don't move from this room until I come for you! Do you hear me, Mona? Don't move from this spot until I come for you!'

"From that point on, I don't know what happened. I don't know who the woman was. I don't know what became of her. I sat in the room with Peter for more than three hours before Father returned. He never again spoke of what happened that day. From that time on, he acted as if those horrible moments on the second floor of our home had never occurred. But one thing did change. From that day until the day he died, he never treated me as he had before that day. In the place of my loving father, a cold, withdrawn man came to take his place. He never hugged or kissed me again. Never smiled at me again. Never told me he loved me. I was an unwelcome prisoner in my own home until I left at seventeen to marry my husband. When Father died, Peter and my mother were at his side, but he wouldn't allow me in the room. Because of my guilt about not listening to my father on that awful day, I've carried this burden my entire life without ever breathing a word of it to anyone…not even my husband. I thought I could bear it alone, but I can't endure the thought of dying without an answer. Why did he hate me for not listening…for trying to protect him? I was just a little girl."

Mona drew a ragged breath, her eyes clouded with anguish. "Who was that dark-haired woman? Why was my father so angry with her? Why did that one moment of disobedience forever change his love for me? Ashleigh, I trust you. I've grown to love you in the years I've been at Rose Manor. You're a kindred spirit and you've become my friend. Help me. Help me to understand the past so I can die in peace!"

Ashleigh struggled to stifle the tears that had sprung to her eyes as she gently stroked Mona's delicate, trembling hands. From behind them, a decidedly not-so-subtle cough abruptly shattered the spell of Mona's words. Mona weakly lifted her head from the pillow on her bed as Ashleigh turned in the direction of the sound.

"Ashleigh, you have other residents to care for. I suggest you move on and finish your rounds." Stephen Roberts, the nursing home director, stood towering in the doorway, gazing at Ashleigh and Mona condescendingly.

As usual, everything about him was perfectly in place – from his dark hair with every strand right where it should be – to the tips of his perfectly polished shoes. As Ashleigh glared into Stephen's smug blue eyes, she bit back a smart remark about to burst from her lips. Only concern for Mona's feelings kept her from letting Stephen know exactly what she thought of his insensitivity.

Ashleigh ignored him as she turned back to Mona. She bent to kiss her cheek, whispering in Mona's ear. "Don't worry, I'll be back. We'll get started on finding your answers right away. I'll do my best to help you. I promise."

As Stephen turned to leave, Ashleigh stood up and tucked the blankets around

Mona's weary body, wondering why Stephen Roberts could annoy her like no other man she'd ever known.

CHAPTER TWO

"Ashleigh, please have a seat." Stephen stood behind his desk, motioning to the chair in front him with a dismissive gesture.

As Ashleigh sat down, she attempted to muster every bit of self-control she possessed. Whenever she became angry, her neck and face turned fire red, and she didn't want Stephen to think he was getting the better of her. Her neck was already damp with perspiration beneath the weight of the long blonde hair covering her neck and shoulders.

Ashleigh could tell by his rigid body language and the terse tone of his voice that this was going to be another one of Stephen's this-is-not-what-you're-here-for lectures. She took a deep breath in a desperate attempt to restrain her temper. She needed to calm down. If she didn't get control of her emotions, this would become a very ugly scene. When Ashleigh suddenly felt several heat spots break out on her neck, she prepared herself for the worst.

She looked around the office to focus on something other than Stephen's patronizing expression. In keeping with his inflexible personality, Stephen's work area was as sterile as it could possibly be. No family photos, no traces of color or beauty – just drab, functional furniture and irritatingly neat piles of paperwork stacked in orderly rows. Stephen folded his hands and coughed, disturbing Ashleigh's reverie.

"Are you catching a cold?" Ashleigh asked with false sweetness. "That's the second time today I've heard that nasty cough."

Stephen's face twisted into a smirk as he unfolded his hands and stared at Ashleigh.

"Must be the chill in this office getting to me," Stephen replied, coughing again for emphasis.

Ashleigh smiled innocently and shot back, her dark eyes alight with fire. "That's a shame. Maybe you ought to take a sick day. You wouldn't want everyone else to catch what you have."

Stephen smirked again but remained quiet as he pulled a stack of papers toward him, flipping through them and studying them as he kept Ashleigh waiting for the inevitable sermonette. "Ashleigh, I've been looking through Mona's records, and as I'm sure you're aware, she's in very fragile health. I heard the conversation between the two of you today and encouraging Mona in fantasies that will only unduly upset her is not a wise course of action at this point in her life. In your capacity as a nurse at Rose Manor, you were not employed to be a friend or counselor to your patients. That's not what you're here for. You were hired to dispense medication, take blood pressure, and to handle medical emergencies. I would recommend that you care for her according to your job specifications and leave the psychiatric care to those who are trained in that field."

As the heat rose from the bottom of Ashleigh's neck to the top of her forehead, she wondered if Stephen would be interested to know that she was a black belt in karate. "Well, I'm sorry, Stephen, but I was under the impression that offering care and compassion to my patients *is* a part of my job specifications. I know you weren't here when I was hired, but if you consult one of those tidy piles on your desk, you'll find that was exactly what the previous director was looking for in a nurse."

Stephen took a deep breath, his eyes never wavering from Ashleigh's glowering stare. "The previous director is no longer here. The facts are that as you idly sit around listening to the dementia-riddled fables of the residents here, you're wasting time and causing a loss of efficiency in the management of this facility. Thus, you're wasting money as well. Please don't make it necessary for me to have to warn you again. The next time I have to speak to you, our conversation will be accompanied with paperwork. I'm sure my meaning is clear."

Ashleigh was speechless with fury as she stood up, her chair rattling noisily on the faux-wood floor. "Your meaning is perfectly clear, Mr. Roberts. If you'll excuse me, I'll get back to work now. I wouldn't want to *waste* any more money." She strode across the room, angrily reaching for the doorknob on Stephen's office door. Before turning the knob, she hesitated, turning to face him. "And please make sure you take care of that cough. You might want to consider seeing a *professional* for it."

***

Turning onto the graveled drive that was his destination every Wednesday evening, Stephen slowed his speed to ten miles per hour as his tires slowly crunched over the limestone gravel. Shifting his Toyota into park, he quickly looked around for anyone that might be lingering nearby. The last thing he wanted to deal with was a chatty stranger who felt any passing visitor was fodder for helping them work through their grief process. Once he determined the coast was clear, he got out of the car and walked the few steps to the gravesite.

As he usually did, Stephen gazed at the headstone for several minutes before finally sitting down in front of it. He reached out and lovingly rubbed his hand over the smooth, grey marble before tracing his fingers over every letter of the engraved inscription. Tears stung his eyes as he glanced around once again to assure himself that he was alone. When he was certain he was, he let the tears fully form and finally spill down his cheeks. Powerless to stop the rising emotion, he opened his mouth to let the sorrow escape, but no sound emerged except the aching groan that told the story of his pain.

He despised himself for his weakness, but even after all the years that had passed, he still couldn't come to terms with how and why he'd lost her. He softly began to whisper the poem he'd found near her body the day she'd died. He had memorized every single word long ago.

"Love comes swiftly

Yet its death dawns slowly

So foolish to think the gift would be given

Even to the lowly

If I am hidden from you

That's the way you want it to be

If I turn and show you my pain

Look for once – let yourself see

You will run

Afraid of the real me

Why do you accuse when I laugh

Instead of crying

Why do you point the finger when I smile

Instead of sighing

You didn't care that I was an illusion

In keeping with your lie

So why would your heart break

If my spirit were to die?

As the words fell silent on Stephen's lips, the need for revenge seethed deep within him. He constantly fought the desire to take justice into his own hands. He'd never bothered with counseling. He knew what they would say. *It's been so many years. By now, you should have worked through the grief process. You should have come to terms with your loss long ago. You need to move on...that's what she would have wanted. You have your memories, and if you have your memories, she's not really gone. You have to forgive all that happened in the past. Hatred will only destroy you, not the person you're hating.*

As true as many of those words might be,

he couldn't do it. He couldn't forgive. And he would never forget. He imagined what a psychiatrist would do with a patient like him if they really knew his innermost thoughts. Probably strap him in a straitjacket and throw him in the closest padded room. Why could no one empathize without feeling the need to talk him out of his pain? He knew by now that some wounds never healed. Why couldn't the world be okay with that?

He rubbed the cool, lush grass beneath his fingertips and wondered if the carpet of green abhorred its job of covering the voiceless lives beneath their roots. When he thought of how she'd loved, his heart ached at the thought of her body being enclosed under the grass and dirt. But his heartache couldn't change what had happened. It was too late. He slowly got up and brushed off his pants, staring pensively at the name on the tombstone. "I'll be back next week. I promise."

***

Stephen shut the apartment door behind him, then hung his keys on the hook beside the door. He threw the single grocery bag on the counter and began thumbing through his mail. Car payment. Phone bill. Fast food coupons. He glanced toward the kitchen window and noticed that the starts for his tomatoes and peppers had gone limp in the unusually sweltering late-May heat. He walked over to the window and grabbed the spray bottle beneath the sill. He began pumping the trigger slowly, carefully misting the small plants. Almost before his eyes, they began to spring back, and as they did, a satisfied smile formed on his lips.

He checked the voicemail on his landline, but as was typical, there were no messages. As he turned away from the phone, a rotund basset hound ambled out of the bedroom, walking slowly toward him. Stephen grinned as he watched the lazy progression. He knew he should stop over-feeding him, but he couldn't bear the basset's morose eyes when he was reduced to a mere cup of dog food per day. He had tried to put him on a diet once but discovered pretty quickly that it just wasn't in him to deny a good meal to the only friend he had on the face of the earth.

He bent down, ruffling the dog's long, droopy ears before rubbing his back. "So how are you today, Bud? Anything exciting happen while I was at work?" Bud's only reply was to roll over on his back, exposing his belly for a rub. "Selfish beast. The only thing you think about is yourself," he said, grinning.

Stephen jumped in surprise as his landline began to ring. He never got phone calls. Not unless it was a telemarketer – and after putting his name on the federal No-Call list, those were even few and far between.

"Hello," Stephen said tersely as he picked up the phone, sitting down on a stool at the bar that divided the kitchen from the living room.

"Hi, Stephen. This is Sarah from work. As you've asked us to do, I'm calling to let you know that Penelope Drake passed away ten minutes ago. Her family has been notified and will be here shortly. We've contacted the funeral director as well. Is there anything else you'd like me to do?"

Stephen paused as he absorbed the news. "Just follow the procedures I've set in place and everything should go smoothly. Thank you for the call."

"Just doing my job," Sarah replied casually.

Stephen nodded. "Well, I appreciate that. Thank you for following the guidelines. See you tomorrow."

As he replaced the phone, Stephen racked his brain for some recollection of Penelope

Drake's face. All that came to the forefront of his mind was her room number...2107. It suddenly occurred to him that Ashleigh would have known exactly who Penelope was. And probably every detail about her life as well.

Shaking his head, Stephen stood up. He grabbed the grocery bag on the counter, heading into the kitchen. Ten minutes later he sat down to a Hungry Man TV dinner and a slice of strawberry pie. He looked down at Bud sleeping beside his chair. "Well, Bud," he said sarcastically, "Happy 31st birthday to me...as if anyone on the planet cares."

CHAPTER THREE

Ashleigh fussed over Mona, first securing the wheelchair, and then tucking the bright pink velour blanket around her legs. The brilliant May sun shone down on the portico, causing the area under the roof to become incredibly warm. Mona leaned slightly forward, reaching toward the planter next to her wheelchair, stroking the delicate violet petals of the flowers. Even the small exertion tired her, causing her breath to become shallow and rapid.

"So beautiful...so...beautiful. Why didn't I take the time to see more...beauty...when I was younger? So busy. Never enough time to notice," she struggled to say, her words trailing into silence.

"Do you need oxygen? Are you sure you're not too warm?" Ashleigh asked, drawing up a seat in front of Mona's wheelchair. She could feel moisture beginning to form at the nape of her neck and down the middle of her back in the eighty-five-degree heat and wondered if Mona could tolerate the unseasonably warm day.

"No, Dear, I'm fine. At my age, I imagine even a one-hundred-degree day couldn't remove the chill from my bones."

Ashleigh smiled, reaching down into her computer bag. She pulled out a legal pad and pen, placing them in her lap. "I wish I had your thermostat. The heat and I just don't get along."

The wrinkled skin of Mona's face creased in layers as she smiled knowingly. "Don't wish for it quite yet. I assure you, it will come soon enough…then the end will be right around the corner," she concluded, her smile disappearing.

Ashleigh reached out and clutched the

trembling hands that were the tell-tale sign of a body assaulted by Parkinson's disease. "Are you positive you have the strength to do this today?"

A curtain of emotion was suddenly drawn over Mona's expressive eyes as she contemplated Ashleigh's question several moments before replying. "Trying to find the answer to what happened that day will put an even further strain on my health, but I must do it. There won't be peace unless I know. I can only hope there will be answers at this late date. For all I know, the truth may lie forever buried with my father in the Eternal Hope Cemetery."

Ashleigh sighed deeply as she clicked her pen, holding it near the top line of the yellow legal pad. "Mona, I made you a promise, and I'm going to keep it to the best of my ability. As you well know, there are no guarantees in life, but I'll give it my best effort, okay?"

The rock-solid resolve returned to Mona's

grey eyes, and she lifted her head slightly, once again ready to fight. "Then let's begin," she said firmly.

"Let's start with your father's full name, his date of birth, and the date of his death."

Mona pursed her lips and looked upward, drawing the statistics from some far recess of her memory. "My father's full name was Richard Jacob Krane. He was born August 2, 1896, in Canton. He was seventy-five-years-old when he died of pancreatic cancer on September 15, 1971. He's buried in the Eternal Hope Cemetery on Middlebranch Avenue here in North Canton."

Ashleigh chewed on the top of her pen as she looked down at the things she'd written on the legal pad. They would be mere words to most people, but this one name and these dates told the story of a past that had broken Mona's child-heart and had clouded the remainder of her adult life. A consuming desire to give Mona closure burned within Ashleigh as she pondered yet again the thought that the lingering questions stood poised to haunt Mona until her very last breath.

Ashleigh had come to cherish Mona deeply in the three years she had been employed at Rose Manor Assisted Care Center. As Ashleigh performed her rounds, she and Mona had developed a bond that had blossomed from an instant connection to an enduring friendship.

With vivacious wit and loving sincerity, Mona had given Ashleigh wise counsel on an array of topics ranging from jealously to the perfect car. In return, Ashleigh became Mona's eyes as she gave the elderly woman a view of the outside world that was no longer accessible to her. Whether it was the never-ending construction on Interstate 77 or the latest account of her sister's deranged boyfriend, Mona never grew weary of the stories that Ashleigh shared with her on a daily basis.

As L.M. Montgomery stated so poetically in *Anne of Green Gables*, a kindred spirit could be found in any size, shape, color, or age, and she regarded Mona as a beloved companion despite the vast difference in their ages. At twenty-seven, Ashleigh suspected many people would never quite understand that she'd found the truest of friends in an eighty-seven-year-old nursing home patient. As she'd watched Mona deteriorate rapidly over the last six months, Ashleigh had been surprised by the deep sorrow that filled her heart as she contemplated the inevitable loss of this amazing woman.

"Alright," Ashleigh continued, abruptly breaking away from her own thoughts. "Tell me what you know of his childhood, his teenage years, and his courtship with your mother, their marriage...all those kinds of things."

A twinge of pain once again marred the features of Mona's face as she reflected on the history of her father's life. "I don't believe he had much of a childhood. His mother died when he was nine, and from that point on, only he and his father were left to run the grocery his father owned on Main Street. It's since been demolished, but for years it was a thriving business. There were four other children, but they were either stillborn or died in early childhood. Of them all, only my father lived to adulthood.'

"Grandfather passed away when I was five, but I have vivid memories of him being a terribly angry man. Nothing was ever good enough, and no one was ever competent enough to satisfy him. He would explode in horrible rages about the smallest things...he terrified my mother. I believe she was secretly relieved when he died. Not a single soul cared when he passed away. We had a simple graveside ceremony. The only people there were Mother, Father and me...Peter hadn't been born yet. Really, I don't know anything about my father's teenage years or any details of his life growing up other than what Grandfather told me about him helping at the grocery store when he was a young boy."

Mona paused, searching her memory for recollections of the past. "I know Father met Mother at a church picnic in 1917 and that they married in January of 1918. I was born shortly after in November of 1918, but other than that, I don't know much. I'm sorry, Ashleigh, I know it's not a lot of information. My parents were both very quiet people, and with the way things were...there wasn't a lot of discussion between us about anything."

As Mona paused to catch her breath, Ashleigh pulled two water bottles out of her bag, opening one and handing it to Mona, then opening the other for herself. It was agonizing to watch Mona try to position the bottle on her lips as her hands moved in opposition to her intentions. Ashleigh looked away as the water dribbled down Mona's chin, having learned long ago that Mona's fiercely independent spirit would not allow her to ask for help.

As Mona patted her chin with a tissue she'd pulled from her flowered smock, Ashleigh smiled. "Ready?" she asked.

"Ready," Mona assured her.

"Okay, before we get back to your father, tell me a little about your mother."

"Oh, she was a wonderful, sweet woman! She was intensely shy and only had a few close friends through the years. She was absolutely devoted to Father, Peter and me. I couldn't have asked for a more loving mother. If it hadn't been for Mother's love, I'm not sure I could have borne the years of silence and disapproval from Father. She was creative. She loved to draw and paint. She never tired of creating beautiful images on canvas. The inspiration for her paintings must have come from a source deep within her, because like most women from that era, she didn't move beyond the sphere of her home and town very often."

"Tell me what happened that evening when your mother came home. How did your father act? Do you think he ever told her what happened while she was away?"

"No, I firmly believe he never told her. We had dinner as we usually did and then mother bathed us and read us our bedtime stories. Father came in and prayed with us as he normally did. I never heard him utter a word or give any indication that something horrible had occurred that day."

Ashleigh slapped the pen down on the legal pad in amazement. "That's just incredible, Mona! How could he have kept it from her? How could he live his life with that kind of secret?"

"I wish I knew."

"Did your mother ever question him as to why he suddenly treated you differently after that day?"

"I heard them talking in the hallway after tucking me into bed. I couldn't hear Mother's question, but I did hear Father say that I had been disobedient. I'm sure she sensed his coldness. It was such a dramatic change. He had been such a loving, caring father up until that day. I cried myself to sleep that night. It was many years before I stopped crying myself to sleep."

"I just find it astounding that she didn't question him further or demand that he change his behavior toward you!"

Mona smiled kindly, as if she were dealing with a very small child. "Women of that generation did not demand of their husbands, Ashleigh. I know in this day and age, you may find that hard to believe, but in that time, it was just the way things were...especially for a woman of my mother's gentle temperament. As I said earlier, I think her way of compensating for Father's aloofness was to shower me with her love. Her love was so precious to me."

"When did you lose her?" Ashleigh asked softly.

Mona visibly flinched. "She died of a massive heart attack two days after my father passed away."

"What?!" Ashleigh gasped. "Oh, Mona, I'm so sorry!"

As the two women once again grasped hands in silent understanding, Stephen unexpectedly walked through the double doors that opened onto the portico. With open-mouthed astonishment, he stopped short as he noticed Ashleigh and Mona together. For a moment he seemed caught off guard, as if he were about to protest, but then noticing Ashleigh's everyday clothes, he abruptly closed his mouth.

Ashleigh smiled up at him, her eyes alight with mischief. "What an incredible day to be off work. Beautiful sunshine, glorious temperatures. You're off tomorrow, right? I hear it's supposed to rain."

"Cute, Ashleigh," Stephen said as he shook his head in disgust and walked away.

As soon as Stephen turned his back, Mona playfully stuck out her tongue at him in protest of his boorish behavior. The two women erupted into giggles as Stephen glanced back and shook his head again.

It was several minutes before they could collect themselves enough to continue, and even then, one of them would burst into laughter as they tried to pursue their previous conversation. After they were finally able to focus again, Mona pulled a photo out of the pocket of her smock and handed it to Ashleigh. "Here's the photograph you asked for. It's the only one I have here at Rose Manor, but Peter's daughter, Connie, has the rest of my pictures and our family records stored at her house if you'd like to see more."

As Ashleigh studied the family picture for several seconds, a chill of foreboding ran up her spine. Gazing at the snapshot of Richard, Sophie, Mona, and Peter Krane on the front porch of Mona's childhood home, she knew beyond a doubt that something was most definitely wrong with the picture.

The front door of the house seemed to call out, beckoning her to step inside to understand the long-buried secrets lying hidden within its walls. The answer to what was wrong with the picture tugged at the corners of Ashleigh's consciousness, but for the life of her, she couldn't put her finger on what it was that was bothering her about it.

CHAPTER FOUR

Ashleigh nervously chewed at her nails as she sat in her car across the street from the immense three-story home. It was most decidedly a monument in brick to the men who had toiled and sweat to build a structure that could withstand the rise and fall of multiple generations.

The home appeared almost exactly as it had in Mona's picture, excepting the addition of black shutters to the many windows. Though the house was large, it had been built on a small city lot. The front yard was nothing more than two small strips of grass on either side of the cement steps leading to the front porch. The flowers lining the walkway and falling luxuriantly from planters attached to the porch were beautiful, leading Ashleigh to the conclusion that someone with a very green thumb lived inside.

Her stomach churned as she mentally rehearsed the speech she'd prepared for the current homeowner. She prayed that the newest resident wasn't a skeptical older person or a young professional like Stephen. Neither type would likely be very sympathetic to her request to see the inside of the home. She had previously decided to give only the skeletal version of events, leaving out the tragic details of the incident Mona had described to her. She would merely relate that Mona was a patient of hers, needing closure regarding her past in this home as she faced an imminent death. She had brought along a camera in the hope that she would be permitted to capture the images of the rooms and the staircase.

As Ashleigh contemplated the difficulty

of the task before her, she found that she was biting her lip so hard she had broken the skin. She took a deep breath, first grabbing her purse and then opening the car door, easing out slowly. The owner would probably think she was a burglar scoping out a place to rob, but it was a risk she had to take for Mona's sake.

Standing on the sidewalk beside her car, Ashleigh gazed across the street at the scene before her. The brick road was lined on both sides with looming two and three-story homes, each as unique as a fingerprint. On either side of the thoroughfare, huge elm trees had grown up and out, reaching for one another across the small expanse of road. The result was a beautifully shaded avenue that made her feel as if she was living in the long-ago past. She smiled, her heart at one with this small slice of fairytale amid modern America.

Taking another breath and finally summoning her courage, she strode across the street and walked up the steps to the front porch of Mona's childhood home. As Ashleigh lifted her hand to knock on the screen door, she was transfixed by the loud wail of a screaming infant. Her heart was beating madly in her chest as she was instantaneously transported back to September 5, 1926. Peter's shrieking cries seemed to pound in her ears as the ebony-haired woman furiously banged on the front door.

Suddenly overwhelmed by a sensation of disembodiment, Ashleigh felt as if she had become the very woman who had stood in this spot nearly a century earlier. She screamed as a little boy unexpectedly jumped up on the other side of the screen door and yelled *Boo!* at the top of his lungs. Ashleigh gasped and stepped backward, frightened out of her wits by the sudden appearance of the preschool goblin. The boy immediately broke into squeals of laughter, falling on the floor and writhing in amusement at her expense.

"Brendon Craig Beecher, what are you doing?" a rebuking voice called from inside the house.

Ashleigh struggled to regain her composure as a slim redhead came to the door with a curly, blonde-haired baby girl straddled on her hip. She looked surprised when she saw Ashleigh standing on the porch, but her smile was pleasant rather than angry.

"Oh, hi! I didn't know anyone was there. Can I help you?"

Ashleigh breathed a sigh of relief at the appearance of the young twenty-something. From the out-of-control curls to the silver nose ring and cut off jean shorts, she was a picture-perfect throwback to the hippies of the sixties. Ashleigh was cautiously optimistic she would have the mindset needed to sympathize with Mona's story.

Still reeling from the effects of the prankster now standing innocently at his mother's side, Ashleigh stammered slightly as she began her prepared speech. "Well...well, you're probably going to find this an unusual request, but I'd like to talk to you about something very important."

The woman cocked her head curiously as the baby on her hip reached up, grabbing a handful of hair, and pulling with all her might. "Ouch! Izzy, stop that!" the redhead yelled.

The incident gave Ashleigh a moment to regroup, and she cleared her throat, beginning again. "I'm so sorry to take up your time. I'm a nurse at Rose Manor Assisted Care Center on Mount Pleasant Road and I have a patient by the name of Mona Carmichael who grew up in this house. She's very frail at this point and it's likely she'll pass away within a few months. She has very vivid memories of her years growing up here, and I would really like to take some pictures of the inside and outside of the home to give her some closure on her past as she faces death. I realize you don't know me, and I know it's a lot to ask to let a stranger into your home. I've brought my diploma from nursing school, my credentials from Rose Manor and a picture of Mona to verify my story. I also have the phone number for Rose Manor if you'd care to call them to verify my employment there."

Ashleigh held her breath as she watched the woman absorb and process her story. She reached into her purse and pulled out her diploma, Mona's picture, and her security badge from the nursing home, offering them to the redhead. To her complete astonishment, the woman ignored them, shocking Ashleigh with a totally unexpected comment.

"Wow, is this amazing karma or *what*? I wonder if the box we found belonged to your patient or someone in her family?" She backed up a step, motioning Ashleigh into the house with her free hand. "Come on in. I'll get the box."

Ashleigh's eyes widened in disbelief as the woman turned and headed into some unknown region of the house. Ashleigh wasn't about to disregard the supposed karma, so she reached for the screen door and opened it, tentatively walking into the living room. The little boy sat down on the floor to play with his trains, but he smiled up at her mischievously first, communicating with his expression that he'd one-upped her with the scene at the door before his mother had arrived. Ashleigh smirked, then smiled to let him know she was really a friend. He seemed satisfied as he set a train down on its wooden track, becoming fully absorbed in supplying the sound effects for his make-believe locomotive.

Ashleigh gazed around the room, her eyes hungrily taking in every detail. The sixties throwback might have a hippie flair to her appearance, but her appetite for expensive furnishings was abundantly obvious. Placed throughout the room were beautifully crafted pieces of workmanship that even Ashleigh's untrained eye could recognize as costly. She looked to the left and saw the brick fireplace that Mona had played before on that fateful day so many years ago. Now, instead of a girl and her dolls, sat a boy and his trains. The Victorian lace curtains on the windows blew softly in the spring breeze, whispering to Ashleigh, urging her to unveil the secrets that had been so inexplicably concealed by Richard Krane.

Straight ahead was the staircase that Mona had described to her. She could hear the redhead rummaging in a room around the corner from the main living area, so Ashleigh quickly tiptoed across the floor and looked up. The stairway was incredibly steep. There were at least twenty steps, maybe more. The thought of the dark-haired woman's descent down this staircase made Ashleigh's stomach churn in revulsion.

The redhead suddenly came bounding into the room with a small, battered box in her left hand. She noticed Ashleigh's position at the steps and smiled broadly. "Isn't it a-ma-zing? It's one of the features I loved best about this house when we were looking into buying it. It's a magnificent staircase...it just *speaks* of the pomp and grandeur of days gone by." She looked upward, smiling at the structure dreamily. "Anyway, come on. Let's sit down."

Ashleigh followed her to a leather couch and took a seat beside her. The woman set the baby down on the floor to play with the scattered trains and blocks. She turned to Ashleigh enthusiastically as she placed the box in her lap. Ashleigh suddenly wished she had Superman's amazing ability to see through objects. "Wow, I really should introduce myself. Sorry! I get carried away sometimes. My name is Rea Beecher. My husband and I have lived here for about a year now. We *love* it here! We just *adore* it!"

"It's nice to meet you, Rea. I really appreciate you being willing to allow me into your home. I can't tell you how much it will mean to Mona. By the way, I'm Ashleigh."

"Wow, do you know your name means meadow of ash trees?"

Ashleigh laughed aloud at the surprising remark. "No, I didn't, but I guess that's better than a meadow of dandelions or something."

Rea giggled, lifting her legs from the floor, tucking them into a pretzel-like Yoga position. "Okay, you told me your story about Mona. Now, I'll tell you my story," she said, rubbing the top of the worn container on her lap. "My husband and I have been doing some remodeling lately...nothing major...just taking care of some rough spots here and there...like updating some things in the kitchen and bathroom. We had some water spots on the walls in the bathroom so a few months ago my husband climbed into the crawl space where all the piping is located to see if it was the source of the water damage. He was a *disaster* when he came out. He looked so cute."

Ashleigh tried to stifle the impatient sigh that was quickly rising to the surface of her lips as Rea began giggling once again, a lovesick stare filling her green eyes. "Wow...there I go again. Well anyway, when he came out he had this box in his hands. Man, I'm getting crazy chills as I'm telling you this." Rea shivered and wrapped her arms around herself dramatically.

Ashleigh wondered if Rea and her husband had traveled to earth on the same spaceship or if they'd made separate flights. Just as she was about to give up hope that the endless commentary would ever cease, Rea lifted the lid of the box and set it to the side. "I don't know...could this stuff have anything to do with your patient or her family?"

Ashleigh's hands were clammy as one-by-one, Rea handed her several objects from inside the container. The first was a yellowed, torn road map of the state of Maine. Ashleigh didn't have time to open and examine it as Rea quickly handed her the second item – a short note written on a piece of very old, flower-bordered stationary. Ashleigh's heart began to race like wildfire as she read the few words written on the fragile paper. Even after all this time, a slight odor of female perfume wafted up and into her nose. Or was it just her imagination playing tricks on her? Ashleigh's eyes pored over every flourish of the delicate female script.

> *My Dear Richard,*
>
> *You may never understand my choice…and it's not one I can expect you to understand. Please hold me in your heart forever. I love you, Richard...I will always love you.*
>
> *Elise*

As Ashleigh looked up in bewilderment, Rea shrugged her shoulders and handed

Ashleigh the last item – a black and white snapshot of a man and woman standing on the shore of an unknown beach. Ashleigh's eyes first traveled to the man, looking for verification that it was indeed Mona's father, Richard Krane. She knew instantly that it wasn't. The man in the picture bore absolutely no resemblance to the picture she'd seen of Richard. Ashleigh's mind whirled in confusion as her eyes traveled slowly to the female standing arm-in-arm with the man on the beach.

From the annals of time, a beautiful woman with one of the most powerfully engaging smiles Ashleigh had ever seen gazed up at her, magnetically drawing her into the spell of the past. Ashleigh gasped as she noticed the woman's free hand buried in a mass of ebony hair, fighting to keep it in place against the power of the seaside wind.

CHAPTER FIVE

"It's not her. I'm sure of it."

Ashleigh shook her head in confusion. Her dark eyes narrowed as she peered at the picture, pointing at the raven-haired beauty again. "Are you sure, Mona? She looks exactly like you described the woman...and then there's the note..."

"I'm certain. I'll never forget her. I've replayed those moments over and over in my mind for eighty years. The madness in her eyes, the fury on her face...it's not something you could forget...even if you tried."

Ashleigh sighed in exasperation as she laid the picture down between them. As she and Mona sat in the library of Rose Manor, *The Wheel of Fortune* droned quietly in the background while Vanna tapped the letter squares and Pat Sajak spun the large wheel. Scattered upon the tables and chairs of the spacious reading room were an array of chess boards, Harlequin Romances, and several knitting projects that residents had abandoned for a snack break in the dining room. Only Ashleigh and Mona remained in the privacy of the now-vacant area.

"Are you alright, Mona? I'm so sorry! Here I am stunning you with the revelation that someone in the past deeply loved your father...and that he apparently was trying to hide that fact...and I haven't even thought to ask how it might be affecting you."

Mona smiled softly at Ashleigh, her eyes tearing up as she looked down at the small box on Ashleigh's lap. "I'm fine, I suppose. Just very confused. I don't know what to make of it all." She extended a shaking hand toward Ashleigh. "May I see the note again?"

Ashleigh reached into the box and held out the delicate stationary. It took incredible effort for Mona to make sense of the words on the worn paper without the cooperation of her trembling hands. She pursed her lips and shook her head in bewilderment as she silently read the few short sentences. "I never once heard the name Elise spoken of in our home..."

"The day your father and the woman were arguing, you said he called her Eunice. Are you sure it was Eunice and not Elise? They both start with an E."

"It seems you're questioning the reliability of my memory," Mona responded with a sly smile.

"Mona, forgive me. I know you've been troubled by these memories your entire life. I have no right to question you."

"Actually, any good investigator would question the memory of an eighty-seven-year-old. I'm teasing you, Ashleigh. But in all seriousness, her name was Eunice. It wasn't Elise," Mona said with conviction.

Ashleigh chewed on her lip, her mind racing. "The picture isn't dated. Based on the clothes and the hairstyles, do you have any idea what year it may have been taken?"

Ashleigh held up the picture for Mona to examine. After several seconds, Mona seemed to have decided. "I would have to place the style of dress in the years somewhere between 1914-1918...during World War I. If you notice, the dress is mid-calf length. That length of dress only became acceptable during the war years when everything from material to food was being conserved. It could have been taken later than that, I suppose, but I would place it in that time-frame. My parents were married in 1918, and in one of their wedding photographs, Mother is wearing a beautiful white dress...and it was mid-calf length."

"Okay, possibly 1914-1918. Let's take a

look at the map." Ashleigh removed the fragile map from the container and carefully unfolded it. She hadn't wanted to open it until she was with Mona out of fear that it would disintegrate in her hands before Mona even had a chance to look at it. It was painstaking work, but Ashleigh was finally able to get the delicate, yellowed map fully opened on the coffee table in front of them without tearing it.

It was immediately apparent to both women that several coastal towns in the southern end of Maine were the focus of the person who had used the map generations earlier. Though now faded by time, the towns of Kittery, Ogunquit, and Saco had been prominently circled in black ink at some point.

Ashleigh looked sideways at Mona with a questioning gaze. Mona shrugged her emaciated shoulders encased in a thick blue sweater. "Kittery, Ogunquit, and Saco," she murmured softly, staring at the map. "The names of those towns mean absolutely nothing to me."

Ashleigh exhaled a deep breath as she leaned forward, tracing her finger along the path of the seaside towns. She wished her intense desire to find the answers to Mona's lifelong questions could automatically solve the perplexing mystery. When she sat back and looked at Mona's haggard face, she could see that as time ticked away, both hope and fear filled her friend's heart.

"There are some avenues I could now explore, Mona. The problem is, we don't even know if this photograph, note, and map are in any way tied to what happened that day. The woman in this picture is not the woman who was at your house, so I'm not sure what to think."

"Let me see the pictures you took of the inside of the house," Mona asked.

Ashleigh reached into her uniform pocket

and drew out the pictures she had taken of Mona's childhood home just the day before. Ashleigh watched as the dreamy, wistful look that had crept over Mona's face when she first told Ashleigh her story once again returned. "It still looks so much the same," she whispered.

"It's a beautiful home," Ashleigh said tenderly.

Mona's brow suddenly furrowed in consternation as she came to the shot of the ascending staircase, rising in grandeur to the second story of the home. She stared hard at the photograph for several minutes as Ashleigh patiently waited. Finally, Mona seemed to come to a decision, and she turned to Ashleigh. "There are two things in my father's life that he seems to have kept hidden...the presence of that woman in our home eighty years ago...and this box. Because of that, I have to believe they're linked. I believe the answers we're looking for will begin and end with this box."

A thrill shot up Ashleigh's spine as a wide smile spread across her face. "I agree with you. They must be connected. I'll do the best I can for you, Mona. I promise."

Their moment of solidarity abruptly came to an end as Stephen appeared in the doorway of the library. He called to Ashleigh, his voice icy with repressed anger. "Ashleigh, if you wouldn't mind, could I talk to you, please."

Ashleigh rolled her eyes in disgust, giving Mona's hand a reassuring squeeze. As she stepped into the hallway to face Stephen, she could feel the familiar heat spots breaking out on her neck. Although at five-seven she wasn't short for a woman, Stephen stood well above her at six-two, making her feel even more vulnerable.

"Ashleigh, I gave you a friendly warning about encouraging Mrs. Carmichael in these delusions, and you have obviously chosen to disregard my instructions –"

"In what part of the world would that have been considered a friendly warning?" Ashleigh shot back, her blood boiling.

Stephen took a deep breath, crossing his arms condescendingly. "Ashleigh, please be in my office at nine tomorrow morning to sign the documentation for your first warning."

Ashleigh's eyes widened in shocked disbelief at Stephen's arrogance. "You've *got* to be joking?"

"Do I *look* like I'm joking?"

"No, that's true, you'd need a sense of humor to be joking," Ashleigh fired back. "You're apparently lacking both that *and* a heart." To her complete mortification, tears began to stream down her cheeks.

For just an instant, Stephen seemed to be shaken at the sight of her tears. "Ashleigh, I'm only trying –"

"Save it. I know the speech. You're trying to run a business here. You don't want the nurse's *wasting* money by sitting around talking to patients who often have no friend on the face of the earth but the people who care for them on a daily basis. That kind of compassion just doesn't make for a cost-efficient establishment. Did I miss anything, Stephen?"

To Ashleigh's astonishment, a pang of deep hurt momentarily crossed Stephen's face, then disappeared almost as quickly as it had appeared. "No, I don't think you missed anything, Ashleigh. I'm a monster, you're *obviously* a saint, and never the twain shall meet." For a moment their eyes locked in piercing intensity, and then he turned away, striding off with the clipped pace of unexpressed fury.

When Ashleigh walked back into the library, her crestfallen face must have clearly articulated the untold the story of the confrontation in the hall. "What? Is everything alright," Mona asked, concerned.

"Oh, everything's fine. Stephen just wanted to inform me that he'll be away tomorrow attending a therapy session for men who have fantasies about ruling the world. Hopefully they'll be able to help him. *I* can't do anything more with him."

The infectious quality of Mona's laughter took hold of Ashleigh, and she quickly forgot she would have to face Stephen again in a little under fourteen hours.

***

Ashleigh tossed and turned as the pursuer chased her down every corridor. The fear was overwhelming as she frantically tried to outrun the shadowy figure following her. Then, with sudden courage, she turned and faced the shapeless form. She stood transfixed as it reached out and handed her a box, then recoiled and melted away. She slowly lifted the lid of the box and reached inside to pull out the snapshot of Mona's family on the front porch of their home. As she gazed down at the photograph, she instantly had the answer to what was wrong with the picture – and just as quickly as she opened her dream-laden eyes, the answer was gone.

CHAPTER SIX

Ashleigh reached into the bread bag and threw the last crumb of bread to the lone duck standing near the gazebo. She watched as fifty more greedy fowl beat a path to join the lucky recipient. She balled up the empty sack and stuffed it into the back pocket of her jeans, pacing restlessly as she waited for her mother to arrive at the park where they'd arranged to meet.

Thanks to Stephen, she was now the proud owner of a written warning in her employment file and foot-loose and fancy-free with a day off without pay. Ashleigh reflected on the terse, short-lived meeting that had taken place between the two of them that morning.

She felt ready for a good round of karate exercises, preferably with Stephen on the receiving end of her kicks. If it weren't for Mona and the other residents at Rose Manor, she would gladly have left her resignation on Stephen's desk instead of a signed warning about her lack of compliance with his instructions.

Ashleigh sighed in relief as she watched her mom's Subaru Outback pull into a spot in the parking lot. As Susan Craig got out of her SUV and pushed the lock button on her key, Ashleigh waved. Susan gave a quick wave in return as she walked rapidly in Ashleigh's direction. As she reached Ashleigh's side, she wrapped her daughter in a huge bear hug.

As they drew apart, Susan's concern was obvious. "Now what's going on? What *happened*?" she asked probingly. When Ashleigh began to explain, her mom took her hand, leading her toward the gazebo. "Wait, let's sit down first."

Once they were seated on the bench in the gazebo, Ashleigh poured out her heart, giving her mother a detailed account of everything that had occurred from the day Mona first shared the unsettling account of her past, to the confrontation between Stephen and herself last night, and the final humiliation in his office at nine that morning. After Ashleigh's story had wound to its conclusion, Susan Craig sat back, exhaling a deep sigh.

"Sweetie, you've had an *interesting* few days, to say the least. The whole thing with Mona is absolutely fascinating…the thing with Stephen…*not* so fascinating."

"What do you think I should do?" Ashleigh asked. "He's absolutely *intolerable* to work for, but I have three years in at Rose Manor, and I love the residents."

Susan smiled knowingly, running her hands through her short, grey-specked hair in a gesture of annoyance. "Part of me would like to smack him. The other part remembers what I always told you as you were growing up..."

"Would that be lecture 364 or lecture 364,000?" Ashleigh teased.

"Oh, aren't you the funny one? With a mouth like yours, just be glad I let you live past sixteen."

Ashleigh smiled at her mom affectionately, finally feeling better after confiding in her. They shared a close relationship, one that had been Ashleigh's anchor through many confusing times.

"As I was *saying*," her mother continued, a glint of humor in her voice. "Like I used to tell you while you were growing up, everyone has a story. Just like Mona...and people like Stephen have a story as well. It's not always the case, but people who seem like complete jerks often have had something happen in their lives to cause them to act the way they do...some deep hurt or pain. Many times, we have to look beyond the surface...we have to care enough to ask questions and delve a little deeper into the lives of the less lovable."

Ashleigh grimaced, but she knew her mom was right. Ten times out of ten, she usually was. "He's less lovable, alright...a little less lovable than a rattlesnake. Are there just some people who aren't worth the emotional effort?" Ashleigh asked.

Susan folded her arms across her chest, giving Ashleigh her most motherly look. "You'll never know until you try."

"I know, Mom. I understand what you're saying, but I can't even *imagine* trying to get to a different point with Stephen. He's just so hard. I don't know how to describe it...it's like there's a fortress around him."

"Sometimes the people that seem the most impenetrable are inwardly begging for someone to have the courage to tear down their walls," Susan said softly.

Ashleigh felt a rush of shame. "I guess Stephen does have one good quality...patience. Despite how disrespectfully I talk to him – which has been quite often lately – he just takes it. After some of the things I've said to him, he could have fired me on the spot. I don't agree with his philosophy regarding Mona, but I do know I've verbally crossed the line with him on several occasions."

"I *don't* doubt that," Susan said, a wickedly humorous smile playing on her lips.

"Is this Bash Ashleigh Day or what? I thought we were here to criticize Stephen," Ashleigh laughed.

"I obviously can't tell you what to do, but if I were you, I wouldn't quit. You've invested in the lives of the people at the nursing home, and most of the time, the big picture is far more important than us as individuals. Those residents need you, and more importantly, you need to learn to walk *through* the tough times in life, not *around* them. If you try to resist pain at any cost, the result will be a lack of character and strength. I bet if you walk through this and don't run away, you're going to come out on the other side with a deep sense of joy and probably some unexpected surprises as well. Life has a funny way of amazing us when we least expect it."

Ashleigh grew quiet as she reflected on the wisdom of her mom's words. Once again, she knew her mom was right. Deep inside, Ashleigh knew staying at Rose Manor was the best thing to do – despite what it might cost her personally. "How'd you get so smart?" she tenderly asked her mom.

Susan leaned over and kissed Ashleigh on the nose, wiping away a stray tear that had fallen just seconds earlier. "Through many excruciatingly hard lessons. Pain always teaches us. That's the beautiful thing about it. I think the wisdom we gain from it is God's way of taking the sting out of something that hurts so much."

"Thanks for coming and talking to me, Mom. I feel so much better."

Susan looked pleased as she slapped Ashleigh's knee in a lighthearted attempt to focus her attention on something other than the horrible morning she'd just endured. "Okay, next topic. I'm dying to talk about Mona's story. It would make for a *great* book, but the problem is, it's real...and according to what you're saying about the state of her health, you're working against the clock."

"I know. I'm kind of panicking," Ashleigh said. "I desperately want to give her an answer so she can finally be at peace. You're the queen of the mystery novel, so I thought you could help. Where should I begin? What avenue should I pursue first?"

As a lifelong lover of mysteries, Susan

was completely in her element as she began instructing Ashleigh in the basics of unraveling a puzzle. "The first thing you have to remember...never assume what you've been told is true. You can be led down many wrong roads because of assumptions. Check out everything. Establish that even the most basic things you've been told are actually true."

"What do you mean? I shouldn't assume Mona's story is true?"

"No, no! What I mean is, don't assume everything you've been told *within* the account of her story is indeed fact. For instance, the date of her father's birth, the date of his death, where he's buried...that kind of thing. Always confirm everything you possibly can. In many of the books I've read, characters inevitably stumble upon information they might otherwise have never uncovered by verifying the most basic information."

"Hmm...interesting. I would never have

even thought about something like that."

"So, where are you going to start with it?" Susan asked, her attention fully engaged by Mona's tale.

"Well, I was going to start with the places in Maine that are circled on the map. The picture of the man and the woman was taken on a beach, and the three towns Richard circled are coastal towns in southern Maine. With the help of the Internet, I should be able to look into what was happening in those towns from 1914-1918...assuming Mona's correct about the dating of the style of clothing they were wearing. Maybe something of interest will crop up in an old newspaper article to lead me in a particular direction...a certain story, a picture...I don't know. I know you told me I shouldn't make assumptions about information I *can* verify, but for right now, I *can't* verify who the woman on the beach was, so I have to assume she's Elise. I don't know why else the snapshot and the note would have been in the box together if the woman in the picture isn't Elise. It seems as if Richard was keeping all his memories of her in one place...her face, the declaration of her love...and possibly her location. Based on that assumption, I thought I could also search the public birth records in Kittery, Ogunquit, and Saco to see if the first name of Elise is listed in any of the files around the time the woman in the picture may have been born."

Ashleigh shook her head, realizing the daunting task that lay before her. "It's going to take a lot of work, because I could run into a list of fifty Elise's...and I also don't know exactly how old she was when the picture was taken. She looks maybe eighteen to twenty-one...approximately. Mona and I both believe that if we find Elise, it will somehow lead us to Eunice."

"Did you bring the pictures?" Susan asked, practically salivating at the thought of holding the pieces of this real-life mystery in her hands.

"Yeah, I did." Ashleigh opened her duffle bag and pulled out the two pictures. She handed them to her mom, watching as she hungrily pored over every detail of the two photographs.

"Incredible," Susan murmured.

"I know...it is."

"I want to give you another bit of advice. Try to track down some relative of Richard's. Any relative at all who may still be living. Even if it's someone like a distant cousin. If there's one thing that holds true about families, it's that they gossip about each other, and that gossip usually gets passed down through the generations in one form or another. A little whisper here, a little story there. If you can find someone like that, you may stumble across something that will help you."

"That's a great idea! I'll check with Mona

to see if her father has any living relatives."

Ashleigh paused, looking down at the picture of Mona's family on the front porch of their home. She pointed to it, asking her mom's opinion. "What do you think of that one? Something about it just seems *wrong*, and no matter how much I wrack my brain, I can't figure out what it is. Does something about it seem wrong to you?"

Susan studied the picture intently, and then looked up into Ashleigh's questioning eyes. "I don't know that I would say there's something *wrong* with it, but there's one thing that definitely stands out to me. Mona's mom and dad and her brother all have light hair...but Mona's hair is *coal black*."

CHAPTER SEVEN

Ashleigh paused at the bottom of the hill
and looked up at the wildflower covered
embankment. The waving spectrum of color
thrilled her senses. She turned toward a large
pond, watching as rays of sunlight dove in, then
burst upward in a crescendo of sparkling light
on the surface of the water.

Ashleigh took a deep breath and lifted her
face to the sun, inhaling the scents of this
majestic bit of nature. The complete isolation,
the water rippling in the wind and the delicate
wildflowers gently blowing in the breeze filled
her with a sense of serenity. She completely
understood why Mona's second cousin, Anna
Miller, had left civilization behind nearly two

decades ago to live atop this knoll that overlooked fifty acres of rugged country.

She smiled before heading up the hillside to the log home she expected to find at the top of the hill. She waded through the sea of flowers, stopping every few seconds to bend down and breathe in their intoxicating aromas. She felt as if she was being carried up the hill by the magical force of this place, and she laughed aloud in childlike wonder as she brushed her hands over the tops of the delicate flowers.

At the peak of the hillside, she found Anna swinging contentedly in a hammock on the front porch of the log cabin. Her legs dangled over the side, propelling her back and forth as she hummed the tune to John Denver's *Country Roads Take Me Home.* The humming was apparently just a prelude because Anna unexpectedly began belting out the chorus in a gravely tenor. "Country roads, take me home, to the place I belong, West Virginia, Mountain

Mama, take me home, country roads..." She stopped abruptly as she spotted Ashleigh watching her from the crest of the hill. She jumped up as fast as her arthritic knees would allow and doubled over in laughter at Ashleigh's amused expression. The exuberant laughter soon turned to a fit of coughing, and the nurse in Ashleigh kicked in as she rushed to Anna's side.

"Anna, are you okay? Let me get you some water!" Ashleigh urged.

Anna Miller's watery eyes were wide as she shook her head in mute exasperation, her cough slowly fading away. "I'm okay...don't fawn over me...there's nothing worse than someone who fawns." She raised an indifferent hand to her cloud of white hair, smoothing its wild, coarse fluff of frizz as best she could. Whole sections stood up in angles completely at odds with one another, one looking like a runway heading straight to the sky and another a looming skyscraper that was about to topple.

It appeared as if it hadn't been combed in years, and neither did it seem as if Anna much cared.

Ashleigh smiled and extended her hand. "It's so nice to meet you! I'm so grateful for the chance to talk to you."

"Well, anyone who's a friend of Mona's is a friend of mine...even if we've never been what you'd exactly call close...but blood runs deep. I'm sorry it's taken as long as it has for you to get out here. I know making arrangements for a visit through letter writing isn't exactly conducive to getting things done quickly, but I have absolutely no use for telephones. They irritate me...destroy my solitude."

She paused as a final cough escaped. "Anyway, I'm not exactly sure what this is all about, but I'll do what I can to help. Mona said you wanted to talk to me about our family. Any particular reason why?" she asked, her dark eyes narrowing into inquisitive slits.

"Well, I'm trying to help Mona solve a

little bit of a puzzle from her past. Something that's important to her."

Anna flashed a sly smile at Ashleigh. "Okay, I get it, this is private stuff. Well, that's okay. I don't want anyone invading my privacy either, so I can respect that. I'll do what I can to help."

Anna opened the front door of the cabin, signaling for the younger woman to follow with an arthritic finger. Ashleigh intuitively knew that despite Anna's rough, no-nonsense exterior, she'd found yet another kindred spirit. She could sense that Anna was that rare person who would do anything for you and one who could carry a secret to her grave. She instantly liked her.

She barely stifled a startled laugh that rose to her lips as she gazed around the small cabin. She'd never seen so much junk piled into one room. In every nook and cranny and every open space on the floor, there were books, boxes, newspapers, magazines, and manila folders stacked in chaotic disarray.

The kitchenette was crammed with unwashed dishes and open jars lying everywhere. The few pictures adorning the walls hung awry, clinging for dear life to the nails that held them in place.

Anna turned and looked at her, laughter brimming in her brown eyes. "Go ahead and laugh. I know you want to. It's okay, I'm not the sensitive type. I'm a pig and I know it. But that's why I'm up here on this hilltop. No one to impress and I live the way I want. Heaven!" She smiled good-naturedly as she walked to the faded couch and removed a stack of books to clear a space for Ashleigh. "Come on, sit down."

"This is a beautiful spot of earth," Ashleigh began after she and Anna were comfortably situated on the worn sofa. "How did you ever find it?"

Anna's eyes took on the same faraway,

wistful look that Mona's did whenever she spoke of the past. "I grew up in Minerva, but my father bought this parcel of land here in Carrollton when I was sixteen. I inherited it from him after he passed away. I built this cabin a few years after he died, and for a long time I used it as a vacation home...but I decided to take up permanent residence twenty years ago this coming August. I just got tired of dealing with the world. Does it sound like a contradiction to say that I really love people, but I just don't want anything to do with them anymore? Now it's just me and my books, and that's the way I like it."

Ashleigh laughed. "I think I know exactly what you mean. I've had a rough couple of weeks, and I'd trade your paradise right now for just about any part of civilization I know of."

Anna smiled at her approvingly, recognizing the spirit of comradeship.

"Well, I know this probably isn't going to

make much sense to you," Ashleigh said, transitioning to why she'd come to Carrollton in the first place, "but what I need is any information you can share with me in regard to Mona's father, Richard. Mona's told me that other than Peter's daughter, Connie, you're the only living relative she has."

"Yes, that's right, we're all that's left. My father's name was Daniel Krane. He and Richard were cousins. My grandfather's name was Jacob Krane, and he and Richard's father, Thomas, were brothers."

"So that would make you and Mona second cousins, correct?"

"It would appear so," Anna jested.

Ashleigh sighed. "Sorry, it all gets extremely confusing as I'm trying to piece everything together from the outside looking in." She paused momentarily, chewing on her lower lip as she looked distractedly around the crowded room, then back to Anna. "Do you know anything at all about Richard's life? Anything?"

"Well, my father and Richard were never close. From what I remember, Richard was a very quiet man, not exactly the type of person who could warm up to others easily. My father Daniel, on the other hand, was a clown. Always the life of the party...very outgoing. He and Richard never really connected on any level. I very much regretted that when I was younger. As an only child, I would have loved to have been closer to Mona...but because of the lack of a relationship between our fathers, we didn't share much of one either. As we grew older, we didn't have much contact. Just life, I suppose. We went in very different directions. I became a reporter for *The Repository*...very unusual for a woman in my day and age," she added proudly, "and Mona devoted herself to her husband Eric. It's a shame they were never able to have children. I know Mona desperately wanted children."

"You can't remember hearing any talk about Richard...anything at all about his past?" Ashleigh probed again.

Anna concentrated, reflecting on the past. "I do remember grandfather saying once that his brother Thomas was a wicked man...that he pitied Richard for having such a depraved father. I'm sorry, Ashleigh, that's all I can think of."

They sat in silence for a few moments before Anna jumped up, suddenly full of enthusiasm. "I can't believe I didn't think of this sooner! Grandfather was absolutely obsessed with our family tree...family history...that kind of thing. He kept a detailed genealogy and written narratives of what history he had in regard to our ancestors. Possibly there's some information in those papers. Anna, what's wrong with you? Are you senile?" she asked herself, smacking her forehead.

Instantly transformed into a woman with the energy of someone half her age, Anna flitted about the room, opening boxes and tearing through papers at lightning speed. She occasionally murmured under her breath as Ashleigh waited on the couch in breathless anticipation.

After fifteen minutes of searching, she held up a worn manila file in her hand, shouting in triumph. "I found it!" She crossed the room quickly, the couch exuding a small cloud of dust as she sat down heavily beside Ashleigh. She scoured the lines of information contained in the genealogies and the accompanying journal accounts about the Krane ancestry. After several minutes of silence, Anna's face suddenly drained of all color, and when she looked up, her expression was one of complete shock.

"Look at this," she said, handing the file to Ashleigh with unsteady hands.

Ashleigh looked down at the yellowed,

tattered papers, her heart pounding in her chest. She could barely believe her eyes when she read the few short lines of narrative regarding Richard Krane that had been written by his decades earlier by his Uncle Jacob.

April 1911 – Richard has disappeared. The family has been in turmoil, while Thomas seems completely unaffected. Almost bitter. He said the 'no good brat ran away.' I pray Richard is safe and that no harm has come to him! Where could he be? Is Thomas telling us the truth?

February 1921 – Richard suddenly reappeared in our lives this month, returning to North Canton with his wife Sophie, and two-year-old daughter, Mona. He won't answer any questions about the ten years he's been gone, and he asked us not to pry into his past. He seems a hundred times the man his father is, and I for one will honor his request. Thank the good Lord he's alive and well!

CHAPTER EIGHT

"Why?" Mona whimpered softly in the pleading tones of a confused child. "Why did they lie to me? Why did *Mother* lie to me? There was no one on the earth I trusted more than Mother."

Ashleigh watched helplessly as tears streamed down Mona's cheeks, her feeble body strained to the breaking point as she absorbed the news that her entire life had been built on a foundation of deceit. Ashleigh pulled a tissue from her pocket and dabbed Mona's face gently. "Mona, don't cry. Please, don't cry," Ashleigh soothed.

Fresh tears fell as Mona lowered her head into her trembling hands, weeping softly. She seemed to crumble as Ashleigh wrapped her arms around the older woman's small frame, holding her tenderly as she whispered reassuringly. "It's going to be alright. I'm so sorry, Mona...I understand...I understand."

The minutes crept by as Mona grew quiet in Ashleigh's arms, her tears eventually subsiding. The ever-present trembling still shook her body, but she was so quiet, Ashleigh thought she'd fallen asleep from emotional exhaustion.

Finally, Mona lifted her head, her stricken eyes boring into Ashleigh's. "How can it be true?" she whispered.

Ashleigh fought to swallow back the fear and the doubt that nagged at her. She wondered if Stephen had been right after all. The rollercoaster of emotions Mona had endured in the last thirty minutes was enough to make Ashleigh question the wisdom of pursuing the ghosts of Mona's haunted past. Ashleigh knew

Mona's reaction had to be sapping what little strength she still possessed. "Maybe we need to let it go, Mona. This isn't good for you."

"No!" Mona said forcefully, her rebounding determination catching Ashleigh off guard. The steel in her eyes returned as she pounded the couch with her fist. "Look around this room, Ashleigh! The pictures of me and my husband. Mementoes of our life together. Peter and his wife and children…the keepsakes from my mother. Now you're telling me that not just that day when a strange woman appeared at our door was kept a secret, but that my *entire life* is shrouded in lies. I have to know *why*! I need answers! Can you understand that?"

Guilt gnawed at Ashleigh as she responded to Mona's insistent plea. "Maybe I missed something. I'm not a private investigator. I could have overlooked something."

Mona vehemently shook her head. "I can

tell by your bloodshot eyes that you haven't missed a single thing. They very clearly tell me how much time you've spent researching every available piece of information. You could possibly have missed one file, but two? No, it's true. I know it's true. Mother and Father *both* lied to me."

To deny it would have been useless. With every minute of her available free time over the past four days, Ashleigh had followed up on the astonishing revelation in Jacob Krane's family narrative. His written account claimed that Mona's father had suddenly disappeared from his home in North Canton, Ohio in 1911 and unexpectedly reappeared in 1921 with his wife Sophie, and his two-year-old daughter, Mona.

Other than today, the most difficult moment of Ashleigh's entire life had been four days earlier when she'd had to tell Mona of her father's disappearance and subsequent reappearance in North Canton.

Mona had adamantly refused to believe that the claims in her Uncle Jacob's papers could be true. She insisted that her mother had many times told her the story of meeting her father at a Presbyterian church picnic during the summer of 1917 and about their wedding on January 5, 1918 in the same Presbyterian church where they'd met. Mona was confident that she and her parents had not suddenly appeared in Ohio in 1921, but that they had been there all along – and that she'd been born in the neighboring city of Canton on November 18, 1918.

She had directed Ashleigh to the personal files she kept in the bottom drawer of a large armoire, where Ashleigh easily located the copy of Mona's birth certificate among the few legal documents she kept stored there. After looking over the official paper that proclaimed Mona's birth, Ashleigh had no reason to believe it wasn't legitimate – but the haunting words in Jacob Krane's papers beckoned her to look beyond the surface.

What reason would Jacob have had to lie? His own words indicated his admiration for Mona's father. Anna had described her grandfather as a jovial man who had been passionate about his hobby of researching the Krane family tree. Ashleigh found no reason to believe there were dark motives involved in the information Jacob had listed about the lives of his extended family.

Faced with two conflicting pieces of evidence, Ashleigh decided to heed her mother's advice about verifying every piece of information given to her. She began by first verifying Richard's birth in 1896. It had taken several hours of searching the archived birth files in the Stark County District Library, but she finally came across the records confirming his birth on August 2, 1896.

Ashleigh's next step had been to substantiate Mona's contention that her parents had been married in North Canton, Ohio. It was during the first hour of this search that Ashleigh's blood began to run cold. It should have been a fairly simple Internet search. The marriage license applications that were listed online went back well beyond the year 1918, and Richard and Sophie's application for a marriage permit should be easily verified.

After an hour of fruitless searching through the 1918 files, Ashleigh had gone through the 1917 files, thinking that Richard and Sophie had possibly filed in December of 1917 before their January 1918 wedding. When nothing came up, Ashleigh scrolled through the entire year of 1917 in a desperate attempt to locate the names of the two people who were swiftly fading into the elusive shadows of an unknown past. She tried 1916. Nothing.

The following two days, she persistently hounded any person in the Canton City Health Department and the Canton City Recorder's

Office who was willing to answer her questions about the record keeping policies of the city. A balding, middle-aged employee for the City Recorder had taken Ashleigh's frantic pleas for help seriously, closely examining Mona's birth certificate.

"It looks authentic as far as I can tell, but it was apparently never filed. If it had been filed, there would have been a record of it. We have extensive records on microfilm from that era which have been transferred to our website. If the woman you're asking about was born in Canton, and you already searched our website, there's no reason why you shouldn't have been able to find proof of her birth fairly quickly."

Ashleigh found sleep a forbidden fruit the night before the inevitable. This morning she had given Mona the devastating news. In the city that was responsible for the record keeping of the smaller environs surrounding it, there was no evidence that Richard and Sophie Krane's marriage had taken place – and absolutely no official record of Mona's birth existed. In a single moment, Mona had been altered from a woman with a very definite past to one whose origins were completely unknown.

***

In the dusky warmth of the early June evening, Ashleigh stood before the gravestone, staring at it contemptuously. The last thing she needed to confirm – and it was validated by the cold stone resting atop the green grass. Richard Krane had indeed died on September 15, 1971. Ashleigh's eyes traveled to the name beside Richard's. Sophie Elizabeth Krane, Born: December 4, 1898, Died: September 17, 1971. She had died two days after Richard's own passing.

Ashleigh sighed heavily. She was physically exhausted and emotionally spent. The past four days had been the most emotionally arduous of her life. She had taunted the past, approaching it with the arrogance of youth, and now it was hunting down her prideful confidence and mocking her. She felt valuable minutes racing by at breakneck speed, and no matter how hard she grasped at them, they ticked away completely beyond her control.

"Why did you do this to her?" Ashleigh cried as she once again focused on the inscription of Richard Krane's name. "You were a coward! It wasn't fair! She was a child! Now, you've taken *everything* from her! I *am* going to find out what you're hiding," Ashleigh said firmly. "There's nothing you've hidden that I'm not going to find. I don't care what you throw at me…I'm going to expose you. I will. I promise you I will!"

Ashleigh shot a final glance of disdain at the tombstone before turning away. Why had Richard and Sophie lied to Mona about the location of their wedding and her place of birth?

As her mind rolled back over the details of Mona's story, Ashleigh recalled Eunice's shock at Mona's appearance in the doorway of her bedroom that fateful day. Mona had said the woman seemed so familiar, yet she was sure she'd never seen her before. Eunice's dark hair. Mona's own coal-black hair. A connection – or merely the happy coincidence of two blonde parents bestowing recessive genes on their daughter? What did it all mean? In which direction did the truth lie and where would she find it now?

Lost in thought as she crested the small hill that led to the gravel drive, Ashleigh stopped short, gasping in shock as she came upon a familiar figure standing before a gravestone directly ahead of her. Tears coursed down his face as grief-stricken sobs wracked his body. Ashleigh stood paralyzed as he lifted his head and stared into her watching eyes. For just a moment there was a bond of understanding between them that went beyond verbal expression. She knew instantly and with complete certainty the kind of man he really was.

"Stephen," she said, inching toward him as he stood unmoving, tears falling onto the front of his shirt.

Suddenly, he stretched out his arm, halting her in place as his face transformed into the expression she knew so well. "No, Ashleigh...don't...please...just don't."

He turned and walked swiftly toward his car as she helplessly watched him go. This time, the tears that fell were not for Mona. They were for Stephen...and for herself.

CHAPTER NINE

Ashleigh sat at the kitchen table tucked into the small breakfast nook, gazing out of her second-floor window. She watched as an elderly couple walking arm-in-arm chatted pleasantly while making a slow progression down the narrow sidewalk.

They paused beneath her window and looked both ways before crossing the street to the historic Canal Fulton Public Library. Ashleigh continued to stare as they slowly made their way up the stone steps to the regal front door of the library. The man released the woman's arm and opened the large door, holding it respectfully as his wife entered the building. The woman smiled, then reached up to affectionately touch his face before she stepped into the building.

` As the door closed behind them, Ashleigh felt tears spring to her eyes. Despite the couple's frail, shuffling movements, it was obvious they were completely in love. The woman's body language signaled her grateful dependence on her husband, and his answering tenderness.

Ashleigh wondered what it would feel like to experience that kind of love. A love that endured decades of change from the first glow of passion to marriage and raising children, to the children growing into adults and finding love of their own. Then grandchildren and great grandchildren, and through it all, a rock-solid devotion that found its true home in the other person's love.

Ashleigh shook her head in aggravation, ascribing the wave of sentiment to the historic magic of this little piece of real estate working on her emotions. Although the more modern areas of Canal Fulton were growing by leaps and bounds every year, the historic downtown area was home to her. She'd been raised in an allotment in Canal Fulton, but had spent innumerable hours in the historic library dreaming of the families that had occupied the stately quarters after its construction in 1880. In 1949, the residence had been converted to a public library, and it had experienced many renovations since that time, with the newest update occurring in 2003.

Despite the changes made through the years, the past was still palpable in the original rooms of the home turned library every time Ashleigh passed through its massive front door.

For as long she could remember, she'd dreamed of owning the older brick home which sat across the street from the library. The home had long ago been divided into an upper and lower duplex, but its vantage point of being located so near the library made it an idyllic spot for her to live. After years of hoping for the impossible, the coinciding circumstances of the property going up for sale and Ashleigh having enough money for a down payment had finally come to fruition two years ago.

After six months of kitchen and bathroom updates and endless general repairs, she had taken up habitation in the roomier upper portion of the home while renting out the lower level to a single mom with a four-year-old boy. Ashleigh was thankful for her ideal situation. Her tenants were relatively quiet and even as they kept their distance out of respect for her privacy, they were friendly neighbors.

In addition to having her dream home, another advantage to her location was that the drive to Rose Manor only took twenty minutes. Just enough time in the car to give Ashleigh the precious moments she needed each morning to mentally prepare for her typically stressful days – and the time she needed at the end of the day to unwind.

Getting up from her chair at the kitchen table, Ashleigh took the last sip of her orange juice before striding into the cozy living room. She looked around the room with a sense satisfaction. For a long time, she'd visualized the homey interior of her home, and to see the picture in her mind become reality was deeply fulfilling. This room especially had become a tranquil oasis in the midst of her busy life. She loved everything from the paintings on the walls to the quaint fireplace to the window seat overlooking the cobbled brick road below. *How many people can say they have a brick road outside of their home?* Ashleigh wondered. She knew her little slice of paradise might not seem like much to most people, but to her it was a dream come true.

A sigh escaped her lips as she tucked herself into the window seat and grabbed a pillow, hugging it against her chest. She'd done a lot of sighing since finding Stephen in the cemetery yesterday. Resting her head against the window, Ashleigh closed her eyes as the brilliant sunlight of the June morning warmed her.

As soon as she shut her eyes, the vision of Stephen's tearstained face and the gut-wrenching emotion of his cries appeared behind her closed eyelids. She let her mind linger on the memory of his pain-softened features and the gentleness of his eyes as he stared at the name on the gravestone. The metamorphosis from the impassive facade that Ashleigh saw every day to the mild sweetness she had witnessed last night was almost beyond belief.

Like she had last night, she realized once again that he was not really the aloof, hard person he tried to portray to the world. That Stephen was trying so hard to hide the presence of such a deep wound stirred something intangible in Ashleigh's heart. She was filled with an overwhelming sense of regret as she realized that by misjudging him so harshly, she might have forever lost the chance to show him true friendship.

After Stephen had left the cemetery and she'd recovered from the shock of finding him there, Ashleigh haltingly made her way to the headstone where he'd stood, bending down to make out the words in the near-darkness. Rebecca Roberts – Born: February 7, 1956, Died: February 14, 1997 – Beloved Mother. The quote below the inscribed words had shaken Ashleigh to her core. *To love as she loved ~ the rarest of joys ~ the greatest of sorrows.*

Ashleigh opened her eyes and thrust the pillow aside. She wrapped her arms around her knees as she struggled to understand the meaning of the words and why someone would have such a chilling epitaph written on a tombstone. She tried in vain to pull her thoughts away from Stephen to Mona and the unanswered questions about her past that were growing more numerous every day.

After thirty minutes had passed into the vacuum of time, Ashleigh stood up in a moment of sudden decisiveness, resolving to push Stephen from her mind in order to focus on the search for Mona's lost history.

***

Stephen found Bud's gurgled breathing intolerable as he lay beside him in the dark. He pushed at the dog, shifting his weight on the pillow to a position he hoped would lessen the sound of the dog's rasping snores. The change made no impression whatsoever as Bud licked his lips in his sleep and resumed the ear-splitting serenade.

Stephen smacked the basset's rear-end in retaliation as he got out of bed and made his way down the hall in the gloom of complete darkness. He sat on the couch in the living room and lowered his head into his hands as the internal war that had consumed him since yesterday continued to rage. The inner turmoil refused to lessen no matter how hard he struggled against it.

He knew that Ashleigh had seen what he'd tried so long to conceal. He'd wanted to reach out to her, but the festering pain called him back, forcing him to hide again beneath the exterior he'd so carefully constructed to protect himself. But as the weeks and months marched on, he found himself growing weary under the weight of the vow he'd made years before. He was tired of the loneliness, yet he was even more terrified of anything that even slightly resembled intimacy. He loved and hated the wall that shielded him all at the same time.

How could anyone ever deal with someone as messed up as me, he wondered. What would be the reward for anyone who tried? Pain. Pain for both of them. He was certain he'd only find rejection. That, or he'd inflict it. Why even try? But the memory of her eyes haunted him as he sat in the shadowy stillness of the dark room. Eyes that told him there was the possibility of a future without pain – if only he could believe them.

***

Ashleigh stood outside Stephen's closed office door as the familiar heat spots crept up her neck – for an entirely different reason this time. She was petrified of what his response would be. She raised her trembling hand to knock and lowered it again. She pressed her balled up fist against her stomach, trying to control the urge to vomit. Finally summoning her courage, she knocked firmly on the door.

"Come in," Stephen called tersely.

Ashleigh took a deep breath, exhaling

slowly as she turned the knob and walked into Stephen's office. He looked up from a pile of paperwork, the pen he held suddenly falling from his hand. He grabbed it again quickly, poising it above the stack of papers in exactly the same posture. As if it had never fallen from his hand in the first place.

Ashleigh managed a nervous smile, looking at the floor as she mentally kicked herself for such ridiculous behavior. She couldn't even imagine what Stephen must be thinking of her presence in his office. He probably thought she was going to berate him for his display of weakness in the cemetery – or that she was going to use what she'd seen to get the written reprimand removed from her employment file. It was a hideous thought.

She'd acted like a fool by never giving him the benefit of the doubt – never trying to understand him. She realized she didn't deserve the chance to start over again, but when she finally gathered enough nerve to look up, she was surprised to find an expression of acceptance on his face. Ashleigh sensed that it took every ounce of strength he possessed to express even that small amount of openness. Her heart swelled and warmed with an emotion that defied description.

"I wanted to talk to you," Ashleigh said softly. She saw him swallow hard, then try to cover it by coughing.

"Okay. About what?"

"About Mona's story."

"What about it?"

"Well, how much did you hear the day she told me about her past?"

"All of it," Stephen said uncomfortably – as if his eavesdropping belied a lack of chivalry.

"Well, it looks as if what she was telling me that day was true. I've done some research into her background and what she told me was just the tip of the iceberg."

"And..."

"I was wondering if you'd want to get some coffee after work and talk through it with me? I'd like to get your thoughts on what I should do next...since you heard it all anyway...if that's okay? It's okay with Mona. I already asked her about discussing it with you. I don't know if you're busy or not..." Ashleigh's voice tapered off into an embarrassed silence as a burning blush crept up her face. She could see the fear imprinted on Stephen's face. It seemed like she suffered a lifetime of humiliation before he finally answered.

"I'd like that. How about Starbucks around 6:30?"

CHAPTER TEN

Ashleigh sat at the small corner table inside Starbuck's, peering out of the large window, looking for Stephen. It was 6:45 and he still wasn't there. As the minutes passed, she grew more upset. *Fifteen minutes isn't a lot*, she reasoned to herself. *He could be tied up in traffic...maybe even caught up with a problem at work.* She tried to convince herself, but she had a definite sense that he wasn't going to show.

She felt as if every eye in the coffee shop was watching her. Ashleigh didn't really care what people might think – she didn't even know any of these people – but the thought that she had sincerely reached out to Stephen and that she might be rebuffed made her unusually paranoid. *You're such an idiot,* she thought to herself. *Fifteen minutes late and you're going off the deep end. Be patient, for goodness sake. Quit jumping to conclusions!*

At 7:30, she was ready to write a dissertation on the perceptive powers of the female mind and its superiority to the inferior psyche of the male gender. She was furious as she walked out of Starbuck's and got into her car. She started it and slammed the gearshift into reverse. She felt like a teenager as she peeled out of the parking lot, the disgusted faces of the sidewalk patrons sipping their iced coffees looming in her rearview mirror.

By the time she'd made it to the intersection of Portage and Whipple, her perceptive female powers were telling her that Stephen had been too terrified to meet her. She knew spite wasn't the reason for his no-show. He was scared to death. She'd read it all over his face in the office that morning as he'd fought between wanting to be kind and needing to protect himself.

As the rush of cars crowded and buzzed past her, a single moment of clarity broke in upon her chaotic thoughts. She knew exactly where to find Stephen. Pausing at a red light, her thoughts altered between resolution and indecision. Would it be right to follow him there, or should she just leave it alone? Something deep within told her he hadn't known real friendship for a very long time, and she wanted more than anything to show him it was possible to experience the kind of friendship that stayed the course.

Ten minutes later, Ashleigh found herself quietly walking up behind Stephen as he sat before the gravestone, his head buried in his hands. She sat down beside him without speaking as the softened brilliance of the evening sun shimmered on the speckled grey marble of the tombstone. She could see the form of Stephen's bowed head reflected in the front of the headstone, and she was overwhelmed by the impression that his life was caught and trapped within the shadow of that tombstone.

Stephen slowly raised his head, looking over at Ashleigh as she sat unmoving on the grass beside him. "I don't know what to say."

Ashleigh returned his steady gaze. "You don't need to say anything."

"Why? Why don't I need to say anything? It was rude not to show."

Ashleigh felt her body tense as some of the coldness with which she was so familiar crept into his voice. "I understand. It's okay."

"Why?" he asked again. "Why is it okay?"

"Stephen, you can't turn back time and act like the other night never happened. You can try, but it won't work. When moments like that change everything, it doesn't do any good to try and reconfigure history. Can't we just be friends now?"

He sighed deeply and ran his fingers through his hair, looking at the ground again. "It may be that easy for *you*, but it's not that easy for me. I'm a mess, Ashleigh. I'm not normal."

"You look normal to me," she teased.

For more than a minute of aching silence, Stephen sat quietly without responding. Ashleigh felt that if she were able to see into his soul, she would be witness to a colossal battle. Personal demons seemed to encircle him, mocking and taunting. The warm night air sparked with their presence, and Ashleigh wanted to deal the death blow that would silence them forever.

"Was she your mother?" she asked, her voice quivering.

When Stephen looked up, unshed tears shone in his eyes. "Yes...she was my mother...she *is* my mother."

"What happened?" Ashleigh asked

tentatively, her heart beating furiously. She knew Stephen would either break or forever retreat under the emotional weight of the question. It was his moment of decision, and she hoped he could free himself from the psychological bondage that imprisoned him.

"It's a long story, and in all honesty, I don't know that I want to go there."

"I'm getting the distinct impression you go there all the time...even if you're not acknowledging that to yourself. It might help to talk about it," Ashleigh urged tenderly.

The expression on Stephen's face betrayed his shock as her dead-on assessment came as a complete surprise. Fear was a raging chaos inside him, but the floodgates of his pain suddenly burst open, and the words poured out as if they had a will of their own. "She committed suicide nine years ago," he found himself saying, his wores echoing the torment he felt.

Ashleigh cringed, the sting of Stephen's grief registering in her own heart. "Stephen, I'm so sorry!"

"She was the most loving person I've ever known. It should have been him...not her," he said bitterly.

"What happened?" Ashleigh asked, trying to negotiate her way through the maze of his conflicted emotions, fearing a wrong move.

Stephen gave a lopsided smile. "Like I said, it's a long story."

"That's okay."

He exhaled a deep breath, gazing broodingly at the cryptic inscription on the gravestone. "When my mom was five, she was taken from her parents and placed into foster care. Her mom and dad were alcoholics and drug addicts. For years, she was bounced back and forth between her parents and different foster homes. Every time her mom and dad completed some kind of rehab program, they'd regain custody of her until they blew it again. The state never tried to sever their parental rights, so she never had the chance to be adopted by a normal, loving family. The pain of those years haunted her. You could always see the hurt in the back of her eyes. But in spite of everything she went through, she had this amazing capacity to love. She was so giving."

"I wish I could have known her."

"She would have really liked you...you're a lot like her."

A burning warmth washed over Ashleigh's body as she fully absorbed Stephen's words.

"She met my dad when she was seventeen and fell crazy in love with him. It was the first time she'd ever experienced love that was reciprocated. She was happy for the first time in her life. They dated for over a year and were inseparable...*until* she told him she was pregnant with me. He didn't want anything to do with a baby...hee left for college and never looked back. He left her alone and pregnant, with no one in the world to care for her. He never apologized...never called when I was born...never sent her a penny of child support. He acted like there had never been anything between them. It was utterly cruel."

Ashleigh shivered, imagining the horrific betrayal. "What did she do?"

"She was amazing! I still can't fathom how she found the strength to do what she did. After my dad abandoned her, she lived at a homeless shelter for several months. The shelter provided programs to help single moms, and somehow, she pulled herself up by the bootstraps and made a life for us. We were poor, but we were happy. We lived in a one room apartment in Canton while she worked on her nursing degree. Eventually, she finished school and was able to get a good paying job at Aultman Hospital. I was twelve before you could say we were anywhere near financially stable…but somehow she always made it work."

"Did she ever get married?"

"Well, that's when everything started to fall apart," Stephen said quietly. Ashleigh watched as he slipped into the past, his face a wall of impenetrable anger as he relived the memories. "Wouldn't you know that Mr. Good-for-Nothing decided to show up again when I was sixteen?"

"Your dad?" Ashleigh asked in amazement.

"Yes, my *father*…if you could call him that. He didn't know what the word meant then, and I don't think he ever will. For all those years my mom and I were everything to each other. It was just me and her. We were a team. When I was little, she would play on the floor with me for hours…she went to all my baseball games…she encouraged me with school…provided for me. Despite all the pain she'd been through in her life, she loved me and everyone around her with so much passion. She was the most selfless person I've ever known."

Stephen paused, his eyes growing cold with suppressed rage. "When I was sixteen, my dad suddenly reappeared in our lives. He begged my mom for forgiveness and told her she was the true love of his life. She tried to resist, but it was hopeless. He'd been her first and only love. I don't think she even considered dating again after he abandoned her. She probably couldn't bear the thought of being rejected again, but when he came back into her life it was just more than she could say no to. All those old emotions came flooding back. It completely overwhelmed her. They married three months to the day after he showed up on our doorstep. I knew from the very beginning he was no good. I saw how he watched other women when she wasn't looking. He's a complete narcissist. It flattered him that she still loved him after all those years. I really think that's the only reason he married her. After five years together, he suddenly decided one day that he'd rather be with the twenty-something lifeguard from the community pool than the woman who'd shown him such unconditional love."

"Oh, no!" Ashleigh gasped.

"Oh, yes," Stephen hissed resentfully. "It broke her in a way I've never seen a person break. She was never the same again. She just couldn't get past the idea that there had to be something fundamentally wrong with her to have been rejected by both her parents and the only man she'd ever loved. She fought the pain for about a year, but it finally won. I found her dead from an overdose a week after I graduated from college."

The burden of Stephen's sorrow hung in the air as tears streamed down Ashleigh's cheeks in the stillness of the now-dark evening.

"I vowed that day to never give myself to anyone the way she had," Stephen said flatly. "There's an instability that consumes a person when they love that deeply."

As his words burned in Ashleigh's ears, his cell phone rang, piercing the darkness. He answered it quickly. "Okay, thank you, Sarah," he said curtly after listening carefully for fifteen seconds.

He snapped the phone shut, then shoved it into his back pocket as he stood up. He reached for Ashleigh's hands, his expression achingly tender as he broke the news. "That was Sarah from work. We need to hurry. They've just taken Mona to the hospital."

CHAPTER ELEVEN

Ashleigh was struck with a feeling of déjà vu as she sat in a chair drawn up to Mona's bedside, once again holding the frail hands as she had several weeks earlier when the secret of Mona's past had been slowly unveiled. The curtains were drawn and the room completely dark except for a small overhead light that illuminated the white board proclaiming the name of the nurse on duty.

Ashleigh watched the red lights of the IV monitor flit erratically across the front of the machine's screen as she gently rubbed her thumbs across the paper-thin skin of Mona's hands. An oxygen mask was fitted over her nose and mouth, slipping every time she moved, leaving the impression of its previous position indented on the soft, wrinkled skin of Mona's face. Her eyes were closed, but Ashleigh could tell it was a fitful rest at best as her eyelids flickered and darted as she slept. The pungent, antiseptic smell of the hospital was all too familiar to Ashleigh as she sat quietly in the murky shadows of the silent room.

The low voices of Stephen and the doctor on call drifted in through the slight opening of the door. Ashleigh found the resonant baritone of Stephen's voice oddly comforting as her emotions alternated between fear and panic while they anxiously waited for Mona's test results.

Before Sarah had contacted Stephen, the nurses at Rose Manor struggled unsuccessfully to stabilize Mona's breathing after a long bout of coughing, immediately calling for an ambulance after her heart rate and blood pressure plummeted drastically. The ER team at the hospital stabilized her with oxygen and several medications.

As the director of Rose Manor, Stephen was listed as a contact on Mona's HIPPA form, so he'd been permitted to see Mona as soon as they arrived at the hospital. To Ashleigh's relief, he immediately called her back to the curtained partition in the ER where she found Mona trembling beneath a warming blanket, its folds engulfing her frail form.

The bloodwork, chest X-ray and other miscellaneous tests that followed Mona's stabilization had proven so exhausting, Ashleigh wondered whether the negatives of doing the tests outweighed the positives. She couldn't shake the sensation that Mona's life was trickling away as quickly as each drop of liquid fell from her IV.

When the two male voices in the hallway faded to silence, Ashleigh waited expectantly for Stephen. She found herself holding her breath, her stomach convulsing as she braced herself for the outcome of Stephen's conversation with the doctor. Instead of Stephen entering the room, she heard him begin a conversation with a woman who was obviously making a concerted effort to keep her voice low. Ashleigh leaned her head toward the door, trying to make out what was being said, but the voices were too hushed to be decipherable. *Probably a nurse*, she thought to herself.

"Dear, you should go home and get some rest."

Ashleigh jerked in surprise, caught off guard by the unexpected sound of Mona's fatigued voice. "What are you doing awake? *You're* the one who's supposed to be resting," Ashleigh chided gently.

"I just suddenly woke up. Has anyone spoken to the doctor yet?" she asked somberly.

Ashleigh fidgeted nervously, her heart racing as she attempted to mask her concern.

"Stephen was talking to him just a minute ago, but I think he's talking to a nurse now."

Mona pursed her lips in the shadowy gloom of the room. "It makes no difference, really. It won't be good news."

"Please don't say that," Ashleigh pleaded, grasping her hands more tightly than she had moments ago.

"I told you a few weeks ago that my life is slipping away. I know there's not much time left, Ashleigh."

"Mona, you can't give up! I haven't found the answer yet. I need more time. Don't give in yet. Fight...please, *fight!*"

Mona's strained smile spoke volumes as she stared into Ashleigh's dark eyes. "I'm trying. I truly am. But time is betraying me. It's the most cunning of all enemies," Mona responded weakly, her eyes fluttering shut as she drifted back into an exhausted slumber.

Ashleigh swallowed, choking back her

pain as the door to Mona's room was slowly pushed open by a petite, grey-haired woman with a bob. Ashleigh guessed she was probably somewhere in her early sixties. The woman tentatively peered in, her face expressing pleased acknowledgement of Ashleigh's presence.

Ashleigh had expected a nurse, but the woman was casually dressed in a pair of jeans and a blue sweatshirt instead of a uniform. Glancing at Mona's bed, she waved noiselessly at Ashleigh, then tiptoed across the room as Ashleigh watched quizzically. When she reached Mona's bedside, Ashleigh stood up and smiled hesitantly.

"Hi, Ashleigh," the woman said in a friendly whisper, extending her hand. "I'm Connie Gainsley, Mona's niece."

"Oh!" Ashleigh smiled. "You're Peter's daughter, right?" Connie nodded while looking over to Mona's sleeping figure. "It's nice to meet you!" Ashleigh said, shaking the woman's outstretched hand.

"Thank you," Connie whispered. "It's so nice to meet you as well! I talked to your boss out in the hall just a second ago. He told me you're a very good friend to Mona as well as an employee at Rose Manor. I appreciate you devoting so much time to her. I don't visit as often as I should. I feel guilty about that a lot of the time, but...well...Mona and I have a bit of a strained relationship."

"Really? She's never mentioned that." Connie seemed concerned, her eyes once again drifting in Mona's direction. "Why don't we talk outside," Ashleigh offered, sensing Connie's apprehension.

"Yes, let's do that," Connie agreed.

As the two women stepped into the corridor, Ashleigh softly shut the door to the room, glancing around for Stephen at the same time. She couldn't see him anywhere in the long passage, and she wondered where he may have gone after talking to the doctor. Connie rightly interpreted Ashleigh's perplexed look and volunteered the information about Stephen's whereabouts.

"If you're looking for your boss, he said to let you know he'd be waiting for us in the visitor's lounge around the corner." Connie's face was etched with worry as she paused briefly then continued. "I'm listed on the nursing home's paperwork as Mona's next of kin, so I was notified as soon as she was transported to the hospital, but I didn't get the message until about an hour ago. I've been in North Carolina all week and drove back today. I feel horrible...I should have been here sooner."

"Don't feel horrible. You were on your way home. There's no way you could have known. There's no reason to feel badly."

Connie sighed heavily, unconvinced. "I guess I wouldn't feel bad if I didn't feel so guilty. It's been a few months since I've visited my aunt. I feel terrible about that."

"Why is it that your relationship is so strained," Ashleigh probed. "I'm sorry if I'm being nosy, but Mona and I are very close. She's told me all about her family, and like I said, she's never mentioned having any issues with you. I can't imagine her having a problem with anyone, really."

Connie shook her head. "I know what you mean. She's a wonderful person. It's a difficult thing to explain. Nothing has ever been said overtly, but it's...it's her manner toward me," Connie stammered, slightly exasperated as she attempted to put the nature of her relationship with Mona into words. "I have to go back some to explain. The trouble in our relationship has its roots in the past. My dad, Peter, explained to me long ago that Aunt Mona and Grandpa Richard had a very cold and distant relationship. He could never understand it because his father was a very gentle man and very loving toward him and my grandmother, Sophie. It bothered my dad as a child and continued to trouble him even as an adult."

"Did he ever talk to Mona about it?"

"Yes...well, I should say he *tried* to talk to her about it several times, but Aunt Mona was never willing to go into any depth with him on the subject...but my dad knew beyond a shadow of a doubt that there was something about Aunt Mona's relationship with their father that haunted her."

Ashleigh inwardly fumed, her disgust for Richard Krane growing with every passing moment. "Did he ever talk to his dad about it?" Ashleigh questioned further, suddenly alert to the fact that Connie might be able to contribute information that could help her in unearthing the secrets of Mona's past.

"No, he didn't. He told me it was the greatest regret of his life. He could never find the courage to do it after he overheard a conversation between Grandpa and Grandma when he was ten years old. He said his father seemed so unbending and stern in that conversation that he never had the nerve to brooch the subject with him," she said, the tide of her talkative nature stemmed by the sadness that suddenly clouded her face.

"What did he hear?" Ashleigh pushed, her heart pounding.

"My dad told me that one day Grandpa had been particularly cold toward Aunt Mona, and he'd had enough of it. He'd stewed over it all day and made up his mind to finally confront Grandpa about it. Grandpa and Grandma had gone up to bed, so he went upstairs and marched down the hall as brave as you please, but when he got to their bedroom door, he heard Grandpa speaking angrily. He got down on the floor and listened through the space between the bottom of the door and the floor. My father had never heard his parents argue before that day, so he was stunned by that fact alone…then more so when he heard what Grandpa had to say. He came into the conversation mid-stream, but they were most definitely at odds. He told me Grandma was uncharacteristically insistent. She said, 'Richard, Mona has a right to know! She has that *right*. I don't want to deceive her any longer. This has gone on long enough.' Grandpa was apparently furious. He said, 'It's *my* decision, Sophie, and I'm not telling her! There would be too many questions. Too much confusion. I'm not budging, Sophie. Don't *ever* bring it up again.'"

CHAPTER TWELVE

"Unbelievable," Ashleigh whispered, as she and Connie stood in the deserted hall outside Mona's door. Connie Gainsely would never have guessed the thrill she'd just provoked in Ashleigh with the astonishing disclosure of Richard and Sophie Krane's conversation. "What did your dad think it meant?" Ashleigh asked, struggling to maintain a calm composure in light of Connie's revelation.

Connie blushed profusely, self-consciously pushing a strand of grey hair behind her ear. "You probably think I'm crazy to be telling you all this. What lengths we'll go to in order to justify ourselves when we feel guilty," Connie commented, laughing nervously.

"Somewhere along the line I'll make a point."

"No, I totally understand," Ashleigh assured her, hoping to steer the conversation back to a place where she could gain more information. "Like I said, Mona has told me things about your family, so don't worry. Please, go on."

Ashleigh's heart skipped a few beats as Connie hesitated. Her normal heart rate only resumed again after Connie's bull-in-a-china-shop chattiness kicked back into gear.

"Truthfully, Dad didn't know what to think. He was really just a child when he overheard the conversation, and it didn't make sense to him at all. To think that his very reserved parents were hiding something was almost unfathomable to him. As he got older, he had a theory about what Grandpa was hiding, but he never shared it with Mona. He didn't even tell her about what he'd overheard. He didn't want to cause her more hurt than she'd already endured. At the core of it, he was ashamed as well…he didn't want to admit to Aunt Mona that he'd been afraid to confront Grandpa."

"What was his theory?" Ashleigh questioned, maintaining a casual façade.

"Dad wondered for a while if perhaps Aunt Mona had been adopted. He realized at a certain point that Aunt Mona looked nothing like the rest of the family…and that there was a large gap in age between her and him. He speculated that maybe his parents adopted her before conceiving him. But Aunt Mona was born so shortly after Grandpa and Grandma got married that Dad came to the conclusion that his theory didn't make much sense. He figured most couples would've probably tried for a child at least a couple of years before adopting…especially in that day and age. As it was, Aunt Mona was born less than a year after they married. Like I said, Dad's theory of adoption didn't really seem to make much sense to him after he thought through all of the facts."

"What about her birth certificate?" Ashleigh probed, pumping Connie for more information.

"Yes. That was the fatal blow to his adoption theory. He knew where his parent's kept important documents, and when it finally dawned on him to check her birth certificate, he snuck a look at it one day when Grandma and Grandpa weren't home. It confirmed to him that Aunt Mona was born in Ohio and that Grandpa and Grandma *were* her parents."

Then why was the birth certificate never officially filed? And why did Jacob Krane's family history say that Mona's mom and dad didn't return to the area until 1921, yet the birth certificate Mona claims is hers listed her birth as taking place in Canton, Ohio, on November 18, 1918? Ashleigh thought to herself. It was apparent from Connie's information that Richard and Sophie had maintained their deception with Peter as well as Mona. *Why?*

It was obvious from Connie's revelation that Richard and Sophie had something to hide. But what? Especially in light of the obscure, quiet life they subsequently led. What had happened in their first few years together that would cause them to conceal the truth for a lifetime? An adoption? Even though Peter thought it unlikely, could they have been hiding Mona's adoption after all?

To keep such a secret didn't make sense in 2006, but Ashleigh knew there had been a different mentality about adoption in 1918. Was Mona's birth certificate real and it not being officially filed the result of a clerical error? Had Jacob Krane possibly been senile and confused when he included the entry about Richard returning to North Canton in 1921? But Richard and Sophie had insisted to Mona that they'd married in North Canton – but they had lied.

Was it possible that her birth certificate was a forgery and had never officially been filed for that very reason? Ashleigh felt like a mouse trying to make its way through a maze. Every time she thought she'd found the correct path, she kept hitting walls. She was completely baffled.

Ashleigh suddenly realized the lull in her conversation with Mona's niece. "I'm sorry, Connie. I was thinking about everything you just told me. It seems so strange. I wonder what your grandmother could have been referring to when she said Mona had a right to know, and she didn't want to deceive her any longer."

"No one will probably ever know," Connie admitted sadly. "It caused my dad a lot of heartache that he never knew for certain. Aunt Mona and I used to be very close, but I guess that's when the distancing in our relationship began."

"What do you mean?" As far as she

could see, the fact that Peter was never able to find resolution regarding his parents' conversation had no apparent connection to Mona and Connie's detached relationship.

"Well, let me back up just a little bit again. I'm trying to bring all these pieces together for you, but I'm not doing a very good job of it. I have to start with my dad. I told you that it was the greatest regret of his life that he never confronted Grandpa about his unloving behavior toward Aunt Mona. Dad always felt that one moment where he chose not to face Grandpa became the defining moment of his life. From that point on, he viewed himself as a coward. He hated himself. Guilt about it plagued him even into adulthood. Aunt Mona had never asked him to defend her, but it was something Dad felt any honorable person would have done. It's amazing how episodes from our childhood can overshadow our whole lives," Connie added, her hazel eyes suddenly glazing with tears at the memory of the lifelong pain her father had carried. "Many years after Grandpa died, my dad had what my mom and brother called a 'religious experience.' What I came to understand a short time later was that he had simply become a Christian. In becoming a Christian, Dad understood the truth that Christ had died to forgive sinners, and he was set free from that burden from his past. Because he'd never been able to bring himself to confront Grandpa about Aunt Mona, he was humbled by Christ's courage in going to such a terrible death on the cross to reconcile *him* to *God*. That amazed Dad. Grandpa was already dead, and it was too late for Dad to help him and Aunt Mona repair their relationship, but he was finally able to come to terms with the cowardice he felt he'd shown. He found forgiveness and peace...and he talked to me a lot about that forgiveness and peace, hoping I would find it as well."

Ashleigh felt her face growing flushed as

she became more and more uncomfortable with the religious assertions Connie was making. It was that old politics and religion thing. There were just some things people weren't supposed to talk about.

"I'm sorry if I'm making you uncomfortable," Connie said gently, perfectly comprehending Ashleigh's uneasy expression. Having once been in Ashleigh's position, she was sensitive to the fact that it was difficult to hear someone talk so straightforwardly about their faith. She still remembered how shocked she'd been by her dad becoming a Christian, and how little sense it had made when he first began talking to her about the peace he'd found in knowing Jesus.

"Well...I...I'm just trying to figure out how it all ties together to your relationship with Mona," Ashleigh stammered, her less-than-truthful response pricking her conscience. She glanced down the hall impatiently, wanting nothing more than to finish this conversation.

"It will eventually make sense. Please bear with me a little longer. I became a Christian about a year after my dad first talked to me about his faith. I'll spare you all the gory details, but I'd pretty much made a complete wreck of my life. Two marriages, two divorces…it felt like there was nothing in my life that was truly *real*. Once I knew that I'd been forgiven by God, this unbelievable joy filled me. I was so profoundly thankful that I'd been set free from the guilt of my sin. That's where Aunt Mona *finally* comes in," she teased, her expressive eyes twinkling. "Knowing what had happened in Aunt Mona's life, I wanted her to know she could find that same peace…that she might not have experienced the love of an earthly father, but that she could know the love of God as her heavenly father. I was so full of enthusiasm, and I thought I might be able to help her. I had wonderful intentions, but not the best way of going about it."

Connie smiled ruefully as she reflected on her past behavior. "Through the years I've gained some wisdom, but when I first approached Aunt Mona, I was a little over the top. She listened for a while, but then she abruptly ended the conversation. She told me she didn't want to hear anything more about my new-found faith. Looking back on it, I know I came across as almost accusatory…as if she'd be a fool to not want to experience the same peace I had experienced. She wasn't hateful, but she made it abundantly clear that she wanted nothing to do with God. She asked me to not bring up the subject again. She felt it was nice that I'd found something to believe in, but she didn't particularly care to hear what the Bible had to say about *anything*. Since then, we've had nothing more than a surfacy kind of relationship. I was close to her for so long. The distance in our relationship since has been very hard on me. It's just easier to deal with it by staying away. It sounds terrible, and I know it's wrong, but it's the reality of where we're at," Connie sighed, looking down at the floor.

Ashleigh fought the irrational, insensitive urge to burst out laughing. She could feel a smile forming at the corners of her lips. She turned her head and forced a cough in an effort to hide it from Connie. She could totally relate to Mona's discomfort with Connie's forthrightness. She'd never known a person to be quite so frank in talking about their faith. She knew a few women at Rose Manor who were Christians, and she knew the basics of the Christian faith from her vacation Bible school days as a child, but she didn't feel at ease discussing her personal views about God. Especially with a complete stranger. She was relieved when she saw Stephen rounding the corner at the nurses' station and heading in their direction.

For the first time since Ashleigh had known him, he completely lacked any trace of his usual confidence and aura of superiority. His dark head was down as he walked, his hands buried deep in the pockets of his jeans. He didn't look up until he was within a few feet of them. The expression on his ashen face told Ashleigh all she needed to know. The end of Mona's life was very near.

For several moments, nothing else seemed to exist as he stared at Ashleigh with a warmth and regret that held her suspended in time. As if a movie on fast forward was playing in her brain, image after image rushed before her mind. Stephen's blue eyes. Richard Krane's grave. The ebony-haired woman in the photo clutching her wind-blown hair. Peter wailing in his crib on that fateful day. The body of Eunice lying at the bottom of the steps. The horror-stricken eyes of Mona's doll. The secret love letter from Elise. The cities of Oqunquit, Kittery, and Saco circled on the tattered map that had intentionally been hidden so long ago. It all led somewhere. *But where? Where?* her mind screamed.

"Stephen, I need a leave of absence. I *have* to go to Maine."

CHAPTER THIRTEEN

Stephen and Ashleigh walked in silence through the pre-dawn stillness of the hospital parking garage, the murky, yellow haze emanating from the light fixtures on the cement posts a fitting symbol for the foggy chaos of Ashleigh's thoughts.   When they got to Stephen's car, Ashleigh turned to face him, her deep-brown eyes pleading. "Please, will you tell me now?"

Stephen gazed down at her, hesitating, his blue eyes reflecting a myriad of conflicting emotions. "I only asked to talk to Connie alone out of respect for the fact that she's Mona's family. I wasn't trying to hurt you."

"I didn't think you were trying to hurt

me," Ashleigh said, caught off guard by Stephen's concern and the unnerving tenderness in his eyes. "What made you think that?"

"You seemed angry when you walked away...after I asked to talk to Connie alone."

"I seemed angry?"

"I thought so," Stephen said, a sense of uneasiness creeping over him as the uncomfortable reality of dealing with another person's emotions for the first time in years suddenly hit home.

Ashleigh tore her eyes from Stephen's, glancing down at a jagged crack in the oil-stained floor of the parking deck. "I wasn't angry. I was just...disturbed, I guess."

"By what?"

"Connie was telling me some things about Mona's past, and she was talking a lot about God. It was making me uncomfortable. That's probably why I walked away like I did. I didn't realize I seemed angry. I'm sorry if I gave the impression that I was upset with you."

Stephen shook his head indifferently, the gesture communicating his lack of offense. "Don't worry about it."

A wide grin slowly spread over Ashleigh's face as she absently rubbed her foot across the oil stain on the ground while thinking about Stephen's words. The startled, childlike expression on his face when she looked up was almost enough to cause the smile to burst forth into laughter. *And I once thought he was the big bad wolf!*

"What's so funny?"

"I was just thinking how far we've come from me wanting to show you some of my karate moves a few weeks ago," she laughed.

"It wouldn't have done you any good. I'm a black belt," he said confidently.

"And – so – am – I!" Ashleigh asserted in mock aggressiveness, lifting her chin defiantly.

"Well, mystery of mysteries," Stephen

joked good-naturedly, looking very unconcerned by her challenge. "You never cease to amaze me."

Distracted by the playful banter, Ashleigh was able to forget her exhaustion for a moment, but her smile immediately faded as the reality of Mona's fate once again forced its way to the forefront of her memory, shooting through her thoughts like a bullet.

"So, what did the doctor say?" she asked, her expression gravely serious.

Stephen shifted uncomfortably. "Why don't we get in the car to talk?"

Ashleigh nodded in agreement as Stephen pushed the unlock button on his key. They slid into the car, the Toyota's engine echoing in the cavernous stillness of the parking garage. When he reached to adjust the air conditioning, Ashleigh gently touched his arm. "It's okay. Please just tell me."

Stephen's eyes darted quickly to her hand

resting on his arm, then to her face so full of fear. Ashleigh slowly removed her hand from his arm, waiting.

"It's a lung tumor," he said softly. "The doctor thinks she probably has about a month to live."

Ashleigh stared at him in stricken silence, the magnitude of the diagnosis hitting her like a freight train. "Only a month? A month may not be enough time. I need more time!" Ashleigh leaned forward, burying her head in her hands. Her shoulders began to shake as she cried softly, emotion pouring forth as grief and fatigue finally took their toll.

"Ashleigh, please...don't cry." Stephen stretched out his hand, aching to comfort her. Just as his fingers were about to make contact with her arm, his hand recoiled as if he'd been burnt. The picture of his mom lying in bed and sobbing helplessly rushed before him. The insides of his ears burned with the words he'd said to his mom nine years earlier. *Mom, please...don't cry.* Stephen struggled to maintain his composure as his panic rose. *I can't do this again. I can't do it!*

After a minute, Ashleigh's cries faded, and she pushed her damp blonde hair away from her tearstained cheeks, looking up at Stephen. "Stephen, what's wrong? Are you okay?" she asked, frightened by the paralyzed expression on his face.

"I can't help you," he said woodenly, looking straight ahead.

Ashleigh was stung by his callousness as she stared at him in disbelief. "Well, I..." Her words trailed into silence as she grasped for the words to express her thoughts. Just minutes ago, he'd been teasing her, and now he was acting like a completely different person.

Ashleigh continued to stare at him, not even attempting to hide her confusion. As she sat watching him in the deafening silence he'd induced, comprehension dawned as the sun began to rise and the murky yellow of the garage lights slowly faded in the emerging daylight. "Stephen. I don't need you to save me. I'm sad, but I'm okay. I just need a friend. That's all."

He turned his head and looked deep into her eyes for what seemed like a lifetime. His face gradually softened, and the tenderness she'd seen in the hospital hallway an hour ago replaced the impassive expression that had been there seconds earlier. "I told you I was a mess. Now you know it's the truth."

"You're just human, Stephen. That's all. Just like me and the rest of the people in this crazy world."

He didn't reply but smiled self-consciously as he nimbly shifted the car into reverse. "I know you're exhausted, but I need to ask a favor. Would you mind if we stop by my place before I take you to the cemetery to get your car? It's on the way."

Ashleigh hesitated, puzzled by his request. "You can wait in the car," Stephen offered, sensing her reservation. "I just need to let my dog out. He's used to going out before bed, and I'm sure he's about to burst by now...if he hasn't already," Stephen said with a grimace, imagining the mess that might be waiting for him.

"*You* have a *dog*?" Ashleigh asked, incredulous.

"You find that hard to believe?" Stephen questioned, grinning as an amused smile spread over Ashleigh's face.

"Well...unexpected," she laughed. "What kind of dog?"

"A basset hound."

"A basset hound?" Before she could stop herself, she started laughing uncontrollably.

"And why is that so hilarious?" he asked in mock offense.

"I don't know," Ashleigh said, trying to

stop laughing. "I just can't picture you with a basset hound!"

"Well, you'll soon see that it's the truth. He's quite the character. Has me wrapped around his little paw. He's overweight and every time I try to put him on a diet, he does me in with his eyes. I never follow through, even though I've been lectured by his vet on several occasions."

"What's his name?"

"Bud," Stephen replied nonchalantly, catching the glint of humor in Ashleigh's eyes as they drove through the nearly empty streets.

He turned left off Applegrove Road, steering the car down a drive lined with tall shrubbery and bright orange tiger lilies. An upscale apartment complex composed of several modern buildings was situated to their left, the fronts adorned with black-shuttered windows and small balconies. Stephen pulled to the curb, leaving the car running as he got out. "I'll be right back. It will just take a few minutes."

"Okay, no problem," Ashleigh responded as she sat back contentedly, watching Stephen as he walked toward the first set of buildings, disappearing around the corner.

In less than a minute, he reappeared with the fattest basset hound Ashleigh had ever seen loping blissfully beside him. She leaned forward, gazing out of the windshield. "Definitely not Bud Light," she chuckled. She decided she had to see this in person. She opened the door and got out, walking up to Stephen and Bud. "Well, hello boy," she said, kneeling to scratch behind the dog's droopy ears.

As the hound nuzzled his head into her hands, Stephen grimaced. "He's such a lush," he said, a twinkle lighting his eyes as he watched Ashleigh charm Bud with her attentions.

"Leave him alone," Ashleigh teased. "How would you like it if someone called *you* a lush?"

As Bud rolled over, inviting Ashleigh to scratch his stomach, Stephen grew unexpectedly serious. "Ashleigh, what's really going on with Mona? You know I overheard the whole story that day out in the hall, but you said you've found out more since then. So, what she told you *is* true?"

"As far as I can tell. And from what I've learned since talking to the couple who own her childhood home now and to members of her family…and researching records…the secrets around her past are even more complex than I originally thought they might be. What happened that day when she was little goes far deeper than what Mona may have imagined. I guess I should say that we don't know yet if what I've unearthed all ties together with what happened the day that woman showed up at Mona's home…but there were definitely secrets being kept by her family. A *lot* of secrets…and

Mona and I both feel that somehow they all tie together."

"I feel for her. To know there were secrets like that has to be really difficult."

"I have to find the answer for her, Stephen. That's why I want to go to Maine. Part or all of the answer may be in Maine. If you can get a temp to take my place at work, I really need to do this. I can't bear the thought that she could die not having answers! It would haunt me forever, just like she's been haunted her whole life by what happened that day." Ashleigh looked up at Stephen, silently pleading with him to free her to do what she needed to do.

"Yes, I can get a temp to take your place. But Ashleigh, please promise me one thing...promise me you'll be careful," he said quietly.

A wave of emotion washed over her as Bud got up and put his head on her bent knees, sadly staring up at her face. "I pr-promise," she said, her voice catching at the unexpected expression she discovered in his eyes.

CHAPTER FOURTEEN

The seagull swooped and rose again, hovering in the air before diving once more to land on the pale white sand of Ogunquit beach. Ashleigh smiled at his bird-on-a-mission gait as he padded awkwardly across the damp sand to stand before her, his hard eyes accusing with their unblinking, black stare. She looked past him to the rising sun as its golden hue shone through wispy cirrus clouds as it moved upward to take its triumphant place in the morning sky.

Watching the sun burst into its full splendor moments later, she felt overcome with the same sense of awe she'd known while watching her first ocean sunrise when she was a little girl. She felt like the only adequate greeting for the sublime beauty would be a choir of angels singing the Hallelujah chorus. She could almost hear the melody reverberating across the sky as she absorbed the moment of peaceful solitude, her frenzied thoughts quieted for the first time in nearly three days.

She'd left for Maine on Friday morning, landing at Boston's Logan Airport that afternoon. She'd rented a car and made the ninety-minute drive on Interstate 95 to the quaint, historic town of Oqunquit. From the second she stepped out of her car onto the drive of the Scotch Hill Inn Bed and Breakfast, she'd immediately been enchanted by Oqunquit's coastal charm.

The town's motto of "The Beautiful Place by the Sea" perfectly described the picturesque village that called the Atlantic Ocean its nearest neighbor. Because she'd been so emotionally and physically exhausted from spending Wednesday night at the hospital with Mona, her mom had insisted on making all the travel arrangements for her first stop in Maine. A last-minute cancellation made her stay at Oqunquit's oldest inn during full season possible.

Her mom had been extremely excited about the cancellation, but Ashleigh only fully realized why after she was led through the house and up the staircase to her room. The regal elegance of the old New England home immediately gave her a sense of calm in the storm of urgency that had driven her to Maine.

She sighed deeply as she glanced down at the seagull standing faithfully at his post on the sand, his beady eyes watching her every move. "Is there some reason why you keep watching me?" she asked the bird as a jogger ran by on the nearly deserted beach. He seemed to substantially pick up his pace after encountering a strange woman who talked to birds. The gull finally blinked as if to say, *Ditto for me*, then flapped its wings and swung upward into the sky, soaring gracefully over the lapping waves that crashed onto the shore's soft white sand.

Turning away, Ashleigh regretfully left the sunrise behind and walked briskly toward The Marginal Way, the village's immaculately maintained mile-and-a-quarter footpath that began in town and hugged the rugged, rocky coastline leading to Ogunquit beach. The walkway had long ago become a haven for artists who were inspired to paint the forever-changing Atlantic Ocean.

Halfway up the footpath, Ashleigh sat down on one of the many benches along the pathway to collect her thoughts. Foaming, white-topped waves crashed against the jagged cliffs as she gazed out across the expanse of water. Within two hours, the footpath would be crowded with tourists, but for the moment it was a restive spot that enabled her to review all the questions she'd put down on paper the day before in the Romanesque Revival Oqunquit

Memorial Library.

Ashleigh had fallen in love with the unique stone structure and had learned from questioning the librarian that the library had been built in 1887 through the generosity of faithful summer visitors, George and Nannie Connaroe. She felt guilty for enjoying the appeal of the village as she vainly searched for the obscure ghosts of Richard Krane's past.

After a day of scouring through albums containing historical pictures of the area and reading through newspaper articles dating from 1918 through 1921, Ashleigh left emptyhanded. She'd carefully read every shred of information the librarian was able to come up with – from the Oqunquit society pages of the past to the long-forgotten obituaries of yesteryear. She scanned old photographs of the town with a magnifying glass, hoping to find the brunette beauty named Elise somewhere among the bustling sidewalk crowds.

As she searched for Elise, Ashleigh's mind was continually occupied with the other dark-haired woman she still needed to unmask. Eunice – the person who had forever changed the fabric of Mona's life. In the course of searching for Elise, it suddenly occurred to Ashleigh that she had no clue whatsoever as to Eunice's age or appearance other than the fact that she'd had dark hair.

She had assumed that Eunice had been approximately the same age as Richard Krane, so she'd never thought to question Mona about Eunice's age. Her mother would definitely chide her for that mistake. *Don't assume anything.* Yet, Ashleigh had subconsciously presumed that Eunice had been a relatively young woman because of Mona's description of her ebony hair. She had taken for granted that if Eunice had been an older woman, Mona would have mentioned grey rather than black hair. But what if Eunice dyed her hair or was slow to grey despite her age? What if she'd been wearing a wig?

Was Eunice a young woman or an older woman? It was the first question Ashleigh had written down on a list of questions for Mona. By the end of the day, the list included another substantive question in regard to Sophie Krane. Mona had mentioned her paternal grandfather and the fact that her paternal grandmother had passed away when her dad was only nine, but she hadn't mentioned anything about her mother's parents or extended family.

Since learning of Peter Krane's adoption theory and Jacob Krane's contention that Sophie Krane had arrived in North Canton with Richard in 1921, Ashleigh was now as deeply curious about Sophie's past as she was about Richard's.

What was it that the two of them had so painstakingly hidden from Mona? An adoption? An *illegal* adoption? Was Eunice Mona's mother? Had she possibly been forced to give

Mona up against her will? It had not been uncommon for women living during that era to be pressured into giving up a child born out of wedlock. Had Eunice arrived at Richard's home in 1926 after tracking down her long-lost daughter? If so, in an age of sealed adoption records, how had Eunice known Richard's name? Had they actually known one another at some point?

Had Eunice known Sophie as well? To make things even more complicated, Ashleigh had not yet told Mona about the conversation Peter had overheard between his parents and his dismissed theory regarding an adoption. Out of concern for Mona's health, Ashleigh had decided to keep the information to herself unless it was absolutely necessary to reveal it to Mona. She struggled with gnawing guilt for hiding the news, but she just couldn't subject Mona to any additional pain until she'd discovered the actual truth.

Theory after theory ran through Ashleigh's mind as she tried to make some sense of the convoluted bits of information she'd learned up to this point. Was it possible that Eunice and Richard were connected in some other way and Eunice had absolutely no connection at all to Elise – or Maine – or Mona? But if that was the case, why the malicious laugh when Eunice spotted Mona in the doorway of her bedroom?

Overwhelmed again with a dire sense of urgency, Ashleigh got to her feet and headed up The Marginal Way toward town, impressed with every step by the diverse beauty of the walkway. At one point on the trail, she found jagged rocks bathed in sunlight being sprayed by ocean waves. In another spot, an alcove of brushlike trees shading one of the thirty memorial benches along the footpath. She wondered if she'd ever be able to fully enjoy the town again if she returned, or if the memories of this trip and why she was here would make it an unpleasant place to return to.

Growing warm under the increasing heat of the morning sun, she pulled off her jacket, glad she'd thought to put her long hair in a single braid before leaving the inn. Her mind wandered to Stephen as she trudged along the final leg of the winding footpath. She wondered what he was feeling after the emotional rollercoaster they'd ridden two nights ago. The phone call from Sarah and the long night at the hospital had quickly halted the moment they'd shared in the cemetery. Did Stephen regret baring his soul to her? Was he sitting in Ohio wishing he could take back that moment of vulnerability?

Her heart literally hurt when she thought of how horribly she'd misjudged him and the pain she'd so casually inflicted. She wanted to call in to work to reassure herself that he was okay, but just thinking about it made her nervous. She knew she wouldn't be able to bear it if he answered the phone with the terseness that would tell her he'd retreated behind the wall that had protected him since his mother's death.

Then she wondered why it mattered so much to her. Why she even cared that he might be sorry for having opened up to her. Before she could come to a conclusion, she found herself at the end of the Marginal Way's mile-and-a-quarter trek. Stepping off the path onto Shore Road, she strolled down the sidewalk in search of a restaurant that served breakfast.

After ten minutes of aimless wandering, she found herself in a small, historic section of the old village. She made her way down a narrow alley paved with cobbled grey stones and cloaked by unique red-brick storefronts on either side of the lane. She quickly spotted a small diner to her right, the swinging sign on its rod iron post proclaiming that it served breakfast, lunch and dinner. Ashleigh headed for the tiny restaurant, the old wood door creaking open as she pushed against its impressive weight. She stepped into the dim room and was immediately greeted by the heavenly smell of simmering bacon.

Heeding the *Seat Yourself* sign, she walked toward the back of the restaurant, carefully negotiating the warped, slanted boards of the aged floor. The diner was full of Oqunquit memorabilia – from fishing nets to miniature lighthouses to various painted scenes of The Marginal Way lining the walls. It was apparently one of the old-timer eateries in Oqunquit and Ashleigh slipped into a booth with a sense of appreciation for the history of the town.

Sitting down, her eyes were immediately riveted to the wall beside the booth where a collection of photographs with names beneath each picture was displayed. Ashleigh gazed at the pictures with curiosity, trying to understand their presence in the diner. The people in the photographs were of varied ages. There were children and middle-aged individuals and senior citizens.

To add to her confusion, the photos had obviously been taken at different times. The mixture of black and white and color photos and the various clothing and hair styles represented the unique eras in which they'd each been taken. As Ashleigh's eyes traveled up the wall, she spotted a brass plaque near the top adorned with the simple words *In Memoriam.* Her brows wrinkled in curiosity as she tried to make sense of the collection.

"Hi there! What can I get you?" a young waitress in her early twenties asked cheerfully, interrupting Ashleigh's reverie.

"Oh, hi! Umm...I'd like some scrambled eggs and bacon...and an orange juice, please."

"I'll be right back with that," the curly-haired redhead responded, sauntering toward the kitchen which was now a beehive of activity during the breakfast rush. Ashleigh closed her eyes, feeling weary to the bone. She allowed herself a few moments before forcing them open again. As she did, her eyes came into focus on the printed floral of a woman's dress in one of the pictures scattered across the wall.

As if a bolt of lightning had suddenly struck her, Ashleigh leapt out of the booth and stared at the photograph, dumbfounded. A wave of horror gripped her as she stared at a larger version of the very picture that Richard Krane had hidden in the crawl space of his home so many years ago. Before Ashleigh's eyes was the unknown man and the dark-haired beauty. And beneath the photograph, the words: Rodney and Elise Cavendall.

CHAPTER FIFTEEN

The waitress side-stepped Ashleigh with a wide-eyed stare, sliding the plate of scrambled eggs and bacon onto the booth's tabletop. "Is everything *okay*?" she asked hesitantly as the crazed look in Ashleigh's eyes made her wonder if she should run for her life rather than engaging this woman in conversation.

"Do you know anything about these people?" Ashleigh gasped, pointing to the black and white photo of Rodney and Elise Cavendall.

"No, I have no idea who they are," the waitress answered, backing slowly away. *What in the world is up with this woman?* she thought. *How would I know who they are? That picture is like eons old!*

The apprehensive look in the waitress's eyes finally registered with Ashleigh and she laughed, then tried to explain behavior. "I'm sorry if I'm acting a little deranged. It's a long story, but I have a smaller version of the exact same picture which was recently found in a home that was being renovated in Ohio...and I've been trying to find out who they are," she said, pointing her finger at the photograph again. "And I came into this restaurant for breakfast, and I find the picture *and* their names. It's unbelievable!" she exclaimed in amazement.

The waitress relaxed a little, softening after hearing Ashleigh's explanation for her bizarre behavior. "You found the same picture in Ohio and then you end up discovering who they are *here*? Sounds like fate to me!" the red-head said decidedly. "It must have been meant for you to find them or you would never have come to this particular restaurant."

"I can't believe it," Ashleigh whispered,

staring at the photo, entranced. Only with supreme effort could she tear her eyes from the photo. "Do you know anything about why these different photographs are here? There's a plaque near the top of the wall that says *In Memoriam* and then there are all these pictures. I don't understand."

"The Tin Roof has been around since the early 1900's," the waitress said, referring to the name of the diner. "It's changed hands many times over the years, but the original owner was a fisherman before he opened the restaurant. Because he'd been a fisherman, he had a definite sense of respect for the sea. From what I've been told, he started this wall of pictures years ago to pay respect to the people who lost their lives off the shores of Ogunquit's beaches in one way or another. The tradition has been carried on by the different owners since then. The pictures are usually given to the diner by the surviving relatives. The only one I know anything about is that one," she said, pointing to a photograph of a fair-haired little boy named Jeremy who appeared to be about three years old. "He drowned in about two feet of water on Ogunquit Beach last year. His parents fell asleep in the sun, and he managed to climb out of his playpen and walk into the ocean. It was a huge controversy...why no one noticed him in the water in broad daylight, in the middle of the summer season, no less," she said, shaking her head.

"That's horrible!" Ashleigh said sadly. After a respectful pause, she continued to question the young waitress. "Do you know *anyone* who might be able to tell me about the history of my picture?" Ashleigh asked earnestly.

The girl chewed her lip, thinking. "Well, there's a woman named Frances Dorman who lives down in Perkins Cove. She's ninety-eight and still lives on her own. She was born here and has lived here her whole life, so she knows something about everything that's happened in this area for almost a hundred years. If anyone would know anything about your picture, it would be Frances. She's pretty much an Ogunquit icon."

"Could you give me her address?" Ashleigh asked, her voice shaking with excitement.

"I don't remember the *exact* address, but just ask around down in Perkins Cove. Everyone knows who Frances is. She has a little blue cottage with white shutters."

"Thank you so much!" Ashleigh said while shoving a ten-dollar bill into the waitress's hands. "You'll never know how much you've helped me...and how much you've helped someone who desperately needs answers about her past life!"

"No problem," the red-head said cheerfully as Ashleigh turned, rushing for the door of the diner. "Hey! Aren't you going to eat your breakfast?" she called out.

"No! Go ahead and help yourself!"

"Alrighty, then." Picking up the untouched plate, the young waitress rolled her eyes heavenward, whispering under her breath, "Gee, thanks so much."

***

Fifteen minutes later, Ashleigh was in Perkins Cove, determinedly hunting for Frances Dorman's cottage. The area had originally been called Fish Cove, but its name had been changed to Perkins Cove years before. For decades, the fishermen who gained their livelihood from the sea struggled against its tempestuous moods, dragging their fishing boats ashore each night to protect them from the schizophrenic storms of the Atlantic. The unprotected area had often been devastated by the lack of a breakwater to stay the force of the ocean. In an effort to protect the boats which were their livelihoods, the fishermen eventually formed the Fish Cove Harbor Association in order to purchase the land that would allow them to dig a trench connecting the former Fish Cove with the tidal Josias River.

After its completion, the resulting cove was renamed Perkins Cove. The cove provided a safe harbor in which the fishermen could moor their boats, thus protecting them from the full force of the sea. Since that time, dozens of restaurants and art galleries had sprung up along the shores of the cove, adding personality and life to the very distinct locale.

Ashleigh rushed across one of the town's most photographed features – the manually operated foot drawbridge that spanned the distance of the cove. She came out on the opposite side to an area crowded with older homes. She stopped briefly to breathe in the warm summer air and the charm of the cove.

Vacationers and locals bustled about on the other side of the footbridge and the water was crammed full of small fishing and tourist boats, either moored or making their way out of the cove on tourist expeditions. Ashleigh grabbed the first person who looked like a native – an older man who exuded an air of having been born and bred in Ogunquit. "Excuse me, could you direct me to Frances Dorman's home?"

The man squinted at Ashleigh with piercing grey eyes, sizing her up in a moment, then barked gruffly, "Just a few houses down. Blue and white cottage. You won't be able to miss it. More than likely, she'll be on the front porch."

Ashleigh found the man's words to be totally accurate as she approached Frances Dorman's cottage a few minutes later. The almost-centenarian was rocking contentedly in a white wicker rocking chair on the front porch of her quaint, cove-side cottage. Frances was not at all what Ashleigh expected. She'd never seen a more alert, fashionable ninety-eight-year-old. Clothed in hot pink Capri pants and a yellow t-shirt with coordinating yellow-rimmed sunglasses, Frances smiled welcomingly as Ashleigh approached her home hesitantly.

"Come on up, don't be shy," Frances called warmly.

"I'm sorry to interrupt you," Ashleigh apologized, stepping onto the front porch of the cottage.

"You're not interrupting me," Frances said good-humoredly. "I just sit here and rock all day...except for my lunch and dinner breaks. Sit down and make yourself at home! What can I do for you?" she asked, strangers stopping being a common occurrence for her.

After sitting down in the rocking chair beside Frances, Ashleigh introduced herself.

"My name is Ashleigh Craig. I'm in the area doing some research for a friend of mine. It's a long and complicated story, but my friend is eighty-seven and she's very ill. I'm hoping to find the answers to some troubling questions she has about her past in order to help her...die in peace."

Ashleigh's voice broke as Frances gazed at her, completely absorbed. "A few weeks ago, I was given a picture that my friend and I both believe is connected to the questions she has about her past. When I was at The Tin Roof for breakfast this morning, I found a larger version of the exact same picture hanging on the wall in the restaurant. The waitress there said you might be able to tell me more about the people in the photograph. The names are Rodney and Elise Cavendall."

"Oh, yes!" Frances said, nodding her white head with certainty. "I remember perfectly! When you reach my age, the distant past is somehow easier to recall than the present. Rodney and Elise Cavendall. It was a tragedy," she said, her voice fading into silence.

Ashleigh could barely suppress her excitement as she stared at Frances expectantly. "What happened?"

"Well, I didn't know them personally. I was only eleven at the time...but I remember the events of those few days. Rodney and his wife Elise were in Ogunquit in June of 1919 for a weekend celebration the town was hosting in honor of the men who'd fought in World War I. Rodney Cavendall had been a war hero. I don't remember many of the particulars because I was so young, but like I said, he and a group of other men were here to be honored for their valor in the war. After the celebration on that Saturday, the mayor took Rodney and his wife, Elise, out on his boat Sunday morning. When they hadn't returned by the end of the day, a search party was sent out. The search party found the mayor's capsized boat, but no trace of the Cavendall's or Mayor Jenkins. Apparently, the boat capsized, and they all drowned. Their bodies were never found. It was a tragedy for the entire village."

"Never found?" Ashleigh questioned incredulously. "Their bodies never washed ashore?"

"No, never," Frances answered, lost in the long-ago past.

"You said Rodney and his wife, Elise, were in Ogunquit for the celebration...so they weren't from here?" Ashleigh probed.

"No. They were from somewhere in Maine, but I don't know where. I'm sorry I can't help you more. I remember the incident vividly, but I don't really know anything about the Cavendall's personally," Frances answered, shaking her head.

Ashleigh reached for Frances' hands, squeezing them tenderly. "Thank you *so much*! I cannot express how grateful I am for your help! What you've told me may be a piece I need to solve the puzzle for my friend. Thank you!"

"Well, you're more than welcome, my dear. I'm so happy I could be of some assistance," Frances responded, her eyes sparkling with pleasure behind the yellow-rimmed sunglasses.

***

"Hello, Rose Manor Assisted Care Center. This is Sarah. May I help you?"

"Sarah, this is Ashleigh."

"Oh, hi Ashleigh! How's vacation?"

"Uh...fine," Ashleigh said, deflecting the question. "Sarah, I need you to do me a favor. Is Mona back at the center yet?"

"Yes, the ambulance brought her back from the hospital this morning."

"Okay, great! Please give Mona a

message for me, okay? It's very important."

"Sure, no problem," Sarah said casually.

"Tell her not to give up. Tell her *I've found Elise*."

CHAPTER SIXTEEN

Ashleigh had found Elise, but just as quickly as she'd found her, Elise's beautiful face retreated into the shadows, untouchable and unreachable in the hazy mist of the past.

After talking to Frances Dorman, Ashleigh had immediately headed back to the Ogunquit Memorial Library in search of answers. Surely something as devastating as Ogunquit's mayor and a distinguished World War I veteran and his wife being lost at sea would have been listed in the historical logs she'd searched just the day before.

Yet, she hadn't discovered a trace of the story regarding Mayor Jenkins and the Cavendall's in any of the carefully preserved volumes of local news articles from the pre and post-World War I era. She was confident that if she could find a written account of the event, it would mention Rodney and Elise Cavendall's hometown, and possibly the names of surviving family members. If Ashleigh could only get her hands on that kind of information, it would narrow her search considerably.

Rejuvenated by new-found determination during her walk to the library, Ashleigh was now standing before the demure, middle-aged librarian who'd been so extremely helpful the day before. After listening intently to Ashleigh's question about the absence of any articles regarding the 1919 tragedy in the logs she'd looked through, the librarian asked her to wait while she investigated it.

Ten minutes later she returned, politely regretful as she said, "I'm so sorry. I just got off the phone with the previous librarian who's now retired. He said that two of the historical logs were lost years ago in 1970. They came up missing after a renovation project. At the time, no one took responsibility for their disappearance despite his pleas for answers regarding their whereabouts. Unfortunately, one of those volumes contained extensive newspaper clippings and photographs from the years you're researching. It was one of those situations where someone should have known something, but everyone suddenly becomes ignorant," she said with a disapproving frown.

Ashleigh smacked the counter, unable to contain the frustrated groan that escaped her lips. Nor could she fail to notice the stares of the library's startled patrons as she turned and stormed toward the front door.

***

Famished after the emotionally draining morning, Ashleigh stopped at a restaurant near the library that offered a seafood buffet. She proceeded to unceremoniously stuff herself as she contemplated her next move. The first item on her to-do list was to call Mona regarding the questions about Eunice's age and Sophie Krane's family. It seemed she'd now hit a dead-end in Ogunquit, and the only viable option was to travel the twenty-eight odd miles to the next spot marked on Richard Krane's map – Saco, Maine.

It felt like a timebomb was ticking in her chest as the days quickly slipped through her fingers. Stephen had said the doctor gave Mona only a month to live. Thirty days. If she had thirty thousand days, Ashleigh wondered if they'd be enough to uncover the ghosts that apparently delighted in clothing themselves with invisibility.

***

"Oh, dear, it's so…good…to hear your voice," Mona gasped, her breathing labored.

Holding the cell phone to her ear as she drove down Interstate 95 toward Saco, Ashleigh blinked hard to clear the stinging tears that suddenly clouded her vision. "I miss you, too. You've been on my mind night and day."

"How will I ever be able to thank you for all that you're doing for me?" Mona choked.

"Don't say things like that. You would do the same for me if our situations were reversed. Your job right now is to fight. You have to fight! Did Sarah tell you? I *found* Elise."

There was silence on the other end of the line as Mona struggled to compose herself. "She did. Who was she, Ashleigh? What did she mean to my father?" Mona asked earnestly.

"I'm not that far yet, but I know her full name now. Elise Cavendall. She was married to a man named Rodney Cavendall. The picture of them from your house is a smaller version of a

picture I found here. It was taken on Ogunquit
Beach in 1919 during a celebration the town
hosted in honor of World War I veterans. Both
Rodney and Elise and the mayor of the town
were lost at sea that weekend while they were
on a pleasure cruise on the mayor's boat. Their
bodies were never recovered. Who she was to
your father, I haven't yet discovered. But I'm
getting there, Mona. Just don't give up! I know
we're on the right track. Like you said before,
you know for certain that your father kept two
things secret in his life – the letter and the
photograph of Elise – and what happened in
your home with Eunice in 1926. I believe just as
you do that the two women are somehow
linked. It's only a matter of time before we find
out how."

"It's so unbelievable. You actually found
the same picture in Ogunquit?" Mona asked,
fascinated.

"Yes! It was amazing! I happened upon

it by chance at a local restaurant. I still can't get over it!"

Eyeing the road signs as she made her way down the interstate, Ashleigh paused for several seconds before continuing. "Mona, I need to ask you a few questions that might help me in my research. I can't believe that I never thought to ask you before. One of the questions is about Eunice. How old do you think Eunice was? I know you were only seven and you only saw her for a few seconds, but did you get any impression of her age?"

"Well, that's a strange thing," Mona responded quietly, her mind traveling to the far-away past. "It was a face that seemed somehow...artificial."

"What do you mean?"

"Not young, not old. Does that make any sense?"

"No, it doesn't," Ashleigh laughed. "Can you give me any more than that?"

"If I had to choose, I would say she was an older woman. But only if I had to choose."

"O-kay," Ashleigh said, still confused. "The other question is about your mom."

"My mother?" Mona asked, surprised.

"Yes. I need to understand more about her background for a few reasons," she said evasively, hating the deceit. "You've told me about your dad's parents, but what about your mom's? Did you know her parents...your grandparents?"

"Oh, my," Mona said as she began to cough. "I completely forgot to mention them. I never knew my maternal grandparents. They died in a horse and buggy accident when my mother was nineteen."

"Where did they live?"

"They were from New York," Mona responded as the coughing intensified. "My mother came to Ohio after their deaths to work for the Hoover Company. She met Father shortly afterward. At least that's what she told me growing up," Mona replied, her words heavy with sadness.

"What were their names?"

"Michael and Gwyneth Ross," she answered, the coughing fit beginning to choke her.

Ashleigh heard the raspy barking grow more forceful, reminding her of the stakes. Thirty days to live. "Mona, I need to let you go now. Please promise me you won't stop fighting, and that you'll take care of yourself."

"I promise, dear. I know you're getting close to the truth. I don't care what those doctors say. I'll be here when you get back."

***

"Are you absolutely certain?" Ashleigh asked, flabbergasted.

"Ma'am, this is what I do for a living."

She stepped back, reaching for the bed as her legs gave way and a bead of sweat formed on her upper lip. "Sophie Krane…I mean, Sophie Ross…spent a year in prison in New York for attempted arson when she was nineteen? I'm sorry to keep repeating myself, but you're *absolutely* positive?"

The private investigator Ashleigh had hired to research Sophie Krane's background sighed impatiently. "Absolutely."

She ran trembling hands through her hair, feeling nauseated. After everything else, how was she going to break this news to Mona? "Okay, I understand. Could you fax your report to my attention at The Holiday Inn in Saco, Maine? The fax number is (207)445-2678. Thank you so much for your help."

"You're welcome. Sorry about the bad news," he said.

"Thanks," Ashleigh muttered, her hands now trembling so violently she was barely able to get the hotel phone back on the hook.

Overwhelmed, she curled into a fetal position on the bed as the air conditioner rattled noisily in the background. she tried to make sense of the information she'd been given. Mona's mother had spent a year in prison for attempted arson when she was nineteen. The woman who Mona had described as loving, shy, and creative. A woman who lived the entirety of her uneventful life in North Canton, Ohio, as a housewife never venturing far from her home. It made no sense. Somehow the information had to be wrong. But the odds of that were slim, and Ashleigh knew it.

What were Sophie Krane's secrets and what other types of fire had she and Richard played with before returning to Ohio in 1921? "Oh, God, what am I going *to do*? How am I going to tell her?" she whispered out loud as the muted light of dusk filtered in through the window. As she uttered the words, the image of

Connie Gainsley's sincere face stood out in her mind. *Why am I praying?* Ashleigh wondered to herself, the gnawing truth that she didn't have the right to talk to God in the familiar way Connie could, impressing itself on her.

Suppressing the uncomfortable thoughts, Ashleigh stood up and anxiously paced around the room. After a few minutes, she walked into the bathroom and brushed her teeth vigorously. For no good reason other than she didn't know what to do with all the nervous energy that was running through her.

For a split second, she considered never telling Mona what the private investigator had discovered about Mona's mom…or the mysterious conversation that Peter had overheard. Sophie Krane had suddenly become as enigmatic as either Eunice or Elise Cavendall. What did it mean? How did it fit together – if at all? How could Ashleigh possibly tell Mona about her mother's past? How could she bring herself to do it?

But the searing thought that Mona would consider it another betrayal was more than Ashleigh could bear. After a lifetime shrouded in dishonesty, she knew Mona longed for truth and complete disclosure – no matter how hard it would be to hear. Ashleigh knew she had to tell Mona. She had to tell her *everything*.

CHAPTER SEVENTEEN

Ashleigh gazed across the waters of Old Orchard Beach as the burnished gold of the flaming sunset was reflected off the sea. People milled about, enjoying the summer scenery that would shortly be swept away by the glory of autumn. Couples walked hand-in-hand across the sand, lost in the magic of the lulling waves and the warm saltwater breeze.

A smile tugged at the corners of Ashleigh's lips as she averted her eyes from an adolescent couple to who were obviously having a disagreement. The petite blonde used her index finger like a gun, shooting it for emphasis, while the young man pleaded hopelessly with his fair maiden.

Ashleigh was thankful those hyper-emotional days of puppy love were long past, but she ached for the mature love she saw in the demeanor of the older couples who walked arm-in-arm, deep in conversation or contented silence.

For the first time in a long time, she felt a void in her life. Until recently, she'd been pretty content with being single, but increasingly, the thought of sharing a life with someone and having a family crept into her thoughts. Amid the chaos of the last few weeks, it would have been wonderful to have a strong shoulder to lean on as she struggled to stay afloat above the conflicting emotions that threatened to pull her under. She still hadn't mustered the courage to call Mona. She knew she had to do it. Each moment she put it off caused her to become more edgy and guilt-ridden. She repeatedly reached for the phone, but her fingers felt as lifeless and as stiff as a mannequin's every time she attempted to call Rose Manor.

The PI's report regarding Sophie Krane had arrived, its facts brief and concise, but lengthy enough to terrify Ashleigh for Mona's sake. Confirmed by a copy of her birth certificate, Sophia Lee Ross (a.k.a. Sophia Lee Krane) was born on October 2, 1897 in the small town of Gouverneur, New York, to Michael and Gwyneth Ross. No details of her childhood were available other than the names of the elementary school she had attended and the high school she'd graduated from in the village of Gouverneur.

The private investigator's assertion that Sophie had been convicted of attempted arson in 1916 and released a year later in 1917 was backed up by county court and prison records.

Sophie's parents had indeed died in a buggy accident in 1916, shortly before she was convicted of attempted arson. Copies of their death certificates were supplied for validation.

Knowing she couldn't manage two things at once, Ashleigh had hired the PI to research Sophie's past, but she'd asked for only the basic no-frills background check. Any in-depth investigation into Sophie's history would cost Ashleigh considerably more than she had to spare at this point.

The private investigator had supplied what she'd paid for – facts easily substantiated by public records, but nothing beyond that. A thousand thoughts wound through Ashleigh's mind. A person convicted of attempted arson would usually serve a considerably longer sentence than Sophie had. What factors had come into play to allow such a short sentence for such a serious crime? Was it possible that Sophie's parents had been influential members of Gouverneur society and Sophie was shown leniency considering their untimely deaths?

Later that night, falling into a restless sleep, Ashleigh wondered what other crimes

Sophie Krane might have been capable of committing.

***

Unable to come to any further resolution regarding Sophie for the time being, Ashleigh left for Saco at eight the following morning in search of clues that would lead her to Elise Cavendall's connection to Richard Krane. She traveled to the administrative buildings of York County, into which Ogunquit and Saco were incorporated, once again hunting for a marriage license application – this time for Rodney and Elise Cavendall. The application was a foolproof way to pin down Elise's maiden name.

If she could find her maiden name, she was confident she would be able to track down the roots of Elise's life. Because she had Rodney Cavendall's last name, she searched for his birth certificate, hoping beyond hope that he'd been born in York County. After hours of fruitless investigation through ragged manila files and Internet records, Ashleigh had walked away with absolutely nothing.

She returned to the streets of Saco in vain, wandering for miles. She talked to various locals in search of another Frances Dorman who could supply the elusive piece to her mystery's puzzle, but no such person emerged in the town of nearly twenty thousand people.

Saco was a mixture of nature and manmade beauty rolled into one. Its beaches were gorgeous, while the older areas of the city contained magnificent tributes to Georgian, Federal, Greek, and Victorian architecture, with striking buildings that had been erected during the town's robust manufacturing era. That heyday had come to an end during the 1950's, and in its absence, the city had found a new source of revenue in adding amusement and water parks, focusing on tourism rather than industry. Saco was less quaint than Ogunquit, making it incredibly difficult for Ashleigh to make headway in her search for the story behind the Cavendall's identities.

Frustrated, she made her way to Old Orchard Beach as she had the evening before, hoping to enjoy the solace of the ocean's beauty. She suddenly felt her cell phone vibrate, its noiseless hum indicating she had a call. As she pulled her phone out of her back pocket, she slipped off her sandals and let her bare feet sink into the cool sand.

Her face creased with shock when the name on the caller ID finally registered in her mind. *Stephen?* A chill of fear ran down her spine as she wondered if something had happened to Mona. She knelt in the sand, trying to control her trembling fingers as she punched the talk button. "Hello?"

"Ashleigh, it's Stephen."

"Is Mona okay?" she blurted out,

apprehension causing her to lose all sense of decorum.

"She's fine. She's still here, Ashleigh. I'm sorry if I scared you. As a matter of fact, we just got done reading."

Just as she was recovering from the shock of Stephen's unexpected call, Ashleigh was shocked anew by Stephen's matter-of-fact statement. *"Reading*...with Mona?" she asked incredulously.

"Of course. And you find that shocking?" he teased playfully.

"This sounds amazingly like our Bud-the-dog conversation," Ashleigh responded, sitting down on the sand, flustered but pleased by Stephen's playful banter. "And what were the two of you reading, may I ask?"

"Romeo and Juliet. Mona said she's always wanted to read it. So, I'm reading it to her. I'm enjoying it."

Ashleigh opened her mouth, but shut it

again, completely at a loss for words. She heard Stephen begin to chuckle softly.

"What? Speechless for once?" he asked.

"I know, that's a rarity for either of us," she shot back mischievously.

Stephen laughed, and Ashleigh's heart skipped a beat as the warm vibrancy of it filled her ears. "How's Mona doing?" she asked gravely, switching the subject.

"In my opinion, amazingly well. She's absolutely refused to be subjected to chemo or radiation. She was adamant. There's no missing it when she makes a point. The doctor has her on medication which he hopes will shrink the tumor. It's causing some swelling, but other than that, she seems unaffected for now. Let's just hope the doctor is wrong, and she has longer than he thinks."

"Stephen, thank you for looking after her while I'm gone. It means a lot to me," Ashleigh said, feeling strangely shy.

Stephen cleared his throat as if he were embarrassed. "You're welcome. How's it going in Maine? Mona says you're making some progress."

"I thought I was, but now I'm at a dead-end again. I have one more town I need to visit and I'm just praying," she said, stumbling over the word, "I find what I need to find in Kittery. If I can't track down anything new there, I'm not sure what to do next." She sighed heavily, her threadbare nerves glaringly obvious even over the phone line. "Has Mona talked to you at all about what I discovered in Ogunquit?"

"Actually, she told me everything."

"Are you two going steady all of a sudden or *what*?" Ashleigh laughed. "She's talked to you about *everything*?"

"Mona was really down the day she came back from the hospital. We sat and talked for a long time. I admitted to her that I listened to the conversation between the two of you the day she first told you her story. Right now, she just needs someone to talk to, and since I overheard everything, I think she's kind of looking at me as a stand-in for you while you're away. She filled me in on all the details about what you discovered in Ogunquit. It's amazing, Ashleigh…and the fact that you've been able to learn as much as you have so far is pretty incredible. Keep digging. She's been through a lot of pain in her life…she deserves an answer."

The words cut to the quick as Ashleigh considered the particulars that Mona and Stephen *didn't* know. Once more, the shame of not telling Mona about Sophie's past rushed over her. As the sun was finally swallowed by darkness, Ashleigh felt a curtain draw over her mood as well. "I need to tell you something. There are certain things I've uncovered that I'm afraid will kill Mona if I tell her about them. I'm terrified," she said, her voice breaking.

"I'll do whatever I can to help you,

Ashleigh."

"Thank you," she said gratefully.

After several seconds of silent understanding had passed between them, Stephen spoke again, his voice gentle. "Before you tell me your news, I need to give you a message from Mona so I don't forget. She said that since you asked her the question about Eunice's age, she's been wracking her brain about what seemed artificial about Eunice's face. She's not entirely certain, but she thinks that Eunice's face might have looked artificial because she'd been burned at some point. That would produce scar tissue and make the skin lose its natural elasticity."

With those words, Ashleigh's phone dropped limply from her hand, and she ran to the ocean's edge, vomiting into the waters of the turbulent Atlantic.

CHAPTER EIGHTEEN

Stephen sat the phone down slowly, still stunned. Bud was tightly curled up against his leg, his head perched on Stephen's lap. He cocked one eye open after Stephen set the phone down, as if to say, *That took forever. Can we go to bed now?*

Stephen had just finished talking to Ashleigh, and his mind was reeling. Nothing could have prepared him for the news that Ashleigh had shared or the indecision he felt when she asked his advice about what to do. For more than an hour, they had gone back and forth about whether to tell Mona about the conversation Peter had overheard between their parents and about Sophie's conviction for attempted arson.

When he had mentioned that Eunice's face might have appeared artificial to Mona because of a burn that had healed over, Stephen could have had no idea that he was dropping a bomb in Ashleigh's lap. As they talked, they worked through multiple scenarios and what-if's, finally concluding that the one thing Mona wanted most was honesty – and that she should receive it.

Stephen had repeatedly tried to convince Ashleigh that he would break the disturbing news to Mona, but she'd stubbornly refused. It was when she'd insisted that she should be the one to tell Mona despite the personal pain it would cause her, that Stephen finally acknowledged to himself that he loved her.

Like the beacon from a lighthouse, the truth shone like a single, piercing ray of light, showing the way to a shore whose rocky coastline was filled with danger and fear. But somehow, he knew that the potential for happiness would lay beyond it.

Discomfited, he got up, whistling to Bud. The basset hound stretched and yawned before reluctantly leaving his warm spot on the couch. He followed Stephen out the front door and down the three flights of steps into the stillness of the June night, the stars blazing in the dark sky.

His thoughts were consumed with Ashleigh as he walked along the drive of his apartment complex with his head down and his hands deep in his pockets, Bud strolling lazily at his side. Allowing himself emotional honesty for the first time in years, Stephen admitted that he'd probably loved Ashleigh for quite a while.

After he'd started at Rose Manor, he had quietly watched her from a distance, immediately recognizing that she was different from any other woman he'd ever met. He appreciated her intelligence, her witty sense of humor, and the combination of competence and devotion she lavished on her patients. He'd quickly seen that the residents of Rose Manor were more than a job for Ashleigh. She genuinely cared for every person she came in contact with. Her capacity to love had drawn him to her, yet he'd fiercely pushed back against his own feelings, burying them beneath years of pain. Scanning the night sky with eyes that were now fully open, Stephen realized that his unyielding belief that nothing good could ever last had suddenly become a question instead.

***

Ashleigh sat on the bed in her room at the Holiday Inn staring at the nightstand. She knew if she opened the drawer, she'd find a Gideon Bible inside. Like most people, she had some knowledge of the Christian faith, and if pressed, would probably call herself a Christian. But after meeting Connie Gainsley, Ashleigh realized she didn't possess the certainty of belief or the peace that Connie had spoken of.

At this moment, more than anything, she wanted peace – and she wanted answers to her questions. Why would someone as wonderful as Mona be subjected to a lifetime of pain? Why would Richard and Sophie Krane lie to their daughter? Why was Mona going to die a haunted woman unless Ashleigh could intervene in time? Why was life a jumbled mess of stray ends that never tied together to form a pattern that made any sense?

The war raged within Ashleigh as she reached out, tentatively pulling the drawer open. Would the Bible be able to tell her why, or was it just another book of philosophy in a world that offered no answers? She reached in, pulling out the small brown copy of the Scriptures, holding it in her hands.

Not even knowing where to begin, she

rifled through the pages, letting them fall aimlessly without reading the words. Finally gaining the courage to look down when the pages settled into place, the black print took form before her eyes, the words startling Ashleigh with their unqualified declaration.

Remember this, and be assured; Recall it to mind, you transgressors. Remember the former things long past, For I am God, and there is no other; I am God, and there is no one like Me, Declaring the end from the beginning and from ancient times things which have not been done, Saying, 'My purpose will be established, And I will accomplish all My good pleasure'; Calling a bird of prey from the east, The man of My purpose from a far country. Truly I have spoken; truly I will bring it to pass. I have planned it, surely, I will do it.

Ashleigh's mind whirled in amazement. *Is God really that certain of Himself?* she wondered, astonished by the passages she'd read. *Did he really declare the end from the beginning? If he did, what did that mean for Mona's life, or her life, or anybody's life?* she asked herself, her heart burning in her chest.

She read the words over and over, entranced by their sublime beauty and their unabashed pronouncement of God's power. In the past, Ashleigh had heard multiple visiting pastors to the nursing home quote John 3:16, but she'd never heard anyone mention these verses which were now starkly imprinted on her consciousness.

She glanced to the top of the page which was entitled *Isaiah* in bold capital letters, then at the chapter headings. She'd been reading in the book of Isaiah, chapter forty-six, verses eight through eleven. Settling against the pillows on the bed, she flipped on the overhead reading lamp and paged back until she was at the beginning of chapter one. Like a person who was starving, she hungrily read from the beginning of Isaiah to the end of the book, voraciously consuming every word.

After she finished the last chapter, she turned off the light and lay in the dark, a thousand questions crowding her mind, coupled with a strange new sensation of expectancy.

***

Standing outside the building of the Kittery Historical Society and Naval Museum the next afternoon, Ashleigh gazed at the sign which proudly proclaimed Kittery the oldest incorporated town in Maine. She wandered inside, gazing with appreciation at the many displays tastefully displayed throughout the room. The town of Kittery boasted a rich past, with its founder Alexander Shapleigh having arrived on Maine's shores from England aboard the *Benediction* in 1635. Shapleigh had consequently named the town Kittery in honor of Kittery Court, the English manor home he had left behind in Kingswear at Devon.

Kittery had also long been famous for shipbuilding, the Navy Yard claiming to be one of Kittery's most popular attractions during the 1800's. Replicas of the many ships and schooners built in Kittery reflected the proud history of its maritime past. Ashleigh directed her focus from the interesting displays to the older lady who was working busily at the museum's information desk, her long grey hair drawn into a ponytail fitted with a large red bow at the nape of her neck.

She looks friendly enough, Ashleigh thought to herself, walking slowly toward the desk. "Hello," she said as the woman looked up, a shocked expression lining her smiling, wrinkled face.

"Oh, I'm so sorry, I didn't even see you! I've been searching for something all morning and I'm afraid I was lost in thought. Welcome to the Kittery Historical Society and Naval

Museum," she said cheerfully. "Is there anything I can do to help you?"

"Well, I have a...strange request," Ashleigh faltered, distracted for a moment by the woman's name tag that read: Phyllis Saunders – Director. "I'm looking for anyone who might know something about two people who were lost at sea off Ogunquit beach in 1919. They weren't from Ogunquit, but I have reason to believe they may have *possibly* been from Kittery. I thought the historical society might be a logical place to begin my search," she finished breathlessly, realizing her haphazard explanation probably made no sense whatsoever to the gracious woman behind the desk.

"What were their names, dear?" Phyllis asked, seemingly unaffected by Ashleigh's insecurity.

"Rodney and Elise Cavendall."

Phyllis Saunders closed her bright blues eyes tightly and lifted her head toward the ceiling, concentrating. "I know one of those names. I know that name. Where have I seen that name?" Ashleigh's heart was beating like a cannonball in her chest as Phyllis' eyes suddenly opened with startled certainty. "That's it! Wait here, I'll be right back!" she said, scurrying around the corner to another room.

She returned several minutes later, carrying a small photo album with the words *Haley Farm Road Cemetery* emblazoned on the front of the volume. "I knew I remembered one of the names from the cemetery," Kittery's wide-eyed historical director said with satisfaction. "Because many of Kittery's earliest and most prominent citizens and their ancestors are buried at the Haley Farm Road Cemetery, one of our volunteers recently photographed every marker in the graveyard for reference," she said excitedly, flipping to the center of the album, sliding it toward Ashleigh. "Is this what you're looking for?" she asked, pointing to the picture of a small marble monument with a graceful dove in mid-flight carved above the words that took Ashleigh's breath away.

In loving memory of Elise Marie Cavendall. Born: August 4, 1898, Died: June 15, 1919. One summer I found you ~ One summer I lost you ~ Forever I will love you.

CHAPTER NINETEEN

"There's a monument for Elise, but no monument for Rodney?" Stephen asked.

"Okay, hold on, I'm still looking," Ashleigh said to Stephen as she held the cell phone to her ear, squinting in the sunlight.

She made her way through the old headstones, monuments, and mausoleums, reading the names carefully, amazed by the long-forgotten dates gradually fading from many of the smaller markers. The cemetery, nestled in a shady grove of trees in the countryside on Haley Farm Road, was fairly well maintained, but could use some tender loving care.

"Here's the marker for Elise!" Ashleigh

exclaimed. The small marble monument was tucked under the protection of a large flowering bush which bathed it in a profusion of lavender blooms. "I feel like I'm going to cry," she whispered as she gazed at the words on the headstone. "I felt that way when I first read the words in the album Phyllis Saunders showed me. Being here makes them even more poignant."

Stephen swallowed the lump in his throat as he pictured Ashleigh in the cemetery. He could see her blonde hair flowing down her back and her earnest dark eyes full of sincerity.

"Are you still there? Can you hear me?" Ashleigh asked when Stephen hadn't replied after several seconds.

"I can hear you," he said, clearing his throat. "So, you can't find a marker for Rodney?"

"No. It's not a very big cemetery, and I've looked at the names on every headstone,

monument and mausoleum. Frances told me the
bodies of Rodney, Elise, and Mayor Jenkins were
never found. That means this monument had to
be put here as a memorial to Elise rather than a
resting place for her body. Don't you think it's
logical to assume that a memorial was placed
here by Richard Krane? The final sentence is
worded so similarly to what Elise wrote to him.
She said, *Please hold me in your heart forever.*"

"It seems logical because we know from
Elise's letter that she and Richard were in love.
We know she loved him...and he *must* have
loved her too, or she wouldn't have used that
kind of wording. She apparently thought he
would be upset by whatever choice it was she'd
made. She wouldn't have mentioned his
difficulty in understanding the choice if he
didn't love her as well. But if she loved Richard,
why did she marry Rodney Cavendall? And
why is the monument in Kittery? Who else but
Richard would have put up a monument? Other

than maybe Rodney...but he died with her."

"I know, I know," Ashleigh responded, frustrated beyond description. "There are a thousand unanswered questions! What we do know is that Ogunquit, Saco, and Kittery were marked on Richard's map. Elise died in Ogunquit and there is a monument to her memory in Kittery. That covers two of the spots on the map, although we don't completely understand why the monument is in Kittery. We know that at some point before she died, Richard and Elise were in love, but that she married Rodney Cavendall. We know she made a choice that Richard would never be able to understand. Maybe the choice she had to make was marrying Rodney instead of Richard."

"But why would she do that? And how does it all tie to Eunice and Mona and what happened in 1926? Elise and Rodney died in 1919."

"I don't know, but Mona feels certain that

Elise and Richard's relationship and what happened with Eunice are somehow connected, and despite the lack of evidence to validate it, I feel that way too. I don't know why...I just do. But what if we're wrong? What if I'm chasing rabbits in Maine and the two things aren't connected at all? And then there's Sophie's past and the secret that she and Richard were keeping from Mona. There's just not enough information to bring it all together. I think I'm going to scream! I want to pull every single hair out of my head!" Ashleigh groaned.

"Bald isn't best for everyone. You're beautiful just the way you are. Leave your hair alone," Stephen smiled on the other end of the phone line.

Ashleigh felt her face grow hot, stunned by Stephen's unexpected words. She paused in embarrassed silence, trying but failing to come up with some witty, nonchalant response. "Okay, I will...for now," she stammered, confused, and strangely thrilled at the same time.

"In all seriousness, Mona may be very ill, but her mind is completely intact. I'm learning that more every day. I would trust her instincts. Follow Rodney and Elise, and I'm certain you'll find Eunice as well."

"Follow them…but to where?" Ashleigh took a deep breath as the surreal sensation of being a puppeteer who was desperately willing broken, inanimate puppets to act out a plot they had long ago abandoned, washed over her.

"You know Rodney's last name. Maybe you can track down some of his relatives. Remember, Frances Dorman said she thought Rodney and Elise were from somewhere in Maine, although she didn't know where. It looks like you're going to have to broaden your search. Check the residence listings for all the cities in Maine and enter the name Cavendall. You never know, you might come up with something."

"That's a great idea! I'll call you later and let you know what I come up with. And I still need to talk to Mona about Sophie. I have to do that by tonight or I'll never be able to forgive myself."

"Okay. I'll talk to you later, then. Thanks for calling and letting me know what's happening," Stephen said, his tone resonating with an emotion Ashleigh was afraid to name.

"Alright...bye," she responded as she began to count the minutes until she would talk to him again.

***

After an hour of Internet referencing and cross-referencing, the only Cavendall Ashleigh had come up with was a residence listed in the old money suburbs of Augusta, Maine.

It had taken her several hours to get there,

but driving down the historic and prestigious Winthrop Street, Ashleigh got the uncanny feeling she was in exactly the right spot. Despite the disrepair that some of the older homes had fallen into, the area exuded the kind of privileged affluence that stood above short-lived trends and the passage of time.

The name Cavendall seemed to fit right in among the notable houses that lined both sides of the large thoroughfare. The architecture of each home was incredible, impressing Ashleigh with their various personalities. Longstanding tradition and family pride was apparent from the immaculate lawns and gorgeous flower beds which had obviously been carefully nurtured for generations.

The Cavendall address listed on the Internet was 2645 Winthrop Street. Ashleigh crept along slowly in her rental, thankful for what light was left as she read the numbers on each mailbox. Finally locating 2645, she pulled the car up snugly against the curb, shifting it into park and turning off the ignition.

She was painfully aware that her KIA Rio stuck out like a sore thumb among the Mercedes and BMW's parked in the various drives along the road. The anxiety Ashleigh felt was a thousand times worse than what she'd experienced before knocking on the door of Mona's childhood home – and she didn't expect to find a welcome like the one she'd received from the ditzy but friendly Rea Beecher.

She smiled to herself, imagining the neighbors peeking from behind thick curtains while urgently telephoning the police about the strange woman running loose on Winthrop Street. The fear of being handcuffed and led away to prison spurred Ashleigh to action, and she slid out of her car and walked quickly up the sidewalk and onto the regal front porch of the mansion boasting the Cavendall name. She rang the doorbell, allowing herself no time for cowardice or second-guessing.

Within thirty seconds, a cherubic brunette opened the door, a pleasant smile brightening her face. "Yes, may I help you?"

Ashleigh could barely control the tremor in her voice as she responded. "Uh...yes...uh...are you Ms. Cavendall?"

"Oh, no!" the brunette exclaimed cheerfully, blushing as she clutched the apron covering her white shirt. "I'm just Miss Elizabeth's day help. May I tell her whose calling and what it's in regard to?"

"My name is Ashleigh Craig. If you could let Miss Cavendall know that I'm inquiring to see if she might be a distant relation of Rodney and Elise Cavendall. They passed away many years ago, but I'm trying to find out more about their lives for a friend of mine. It's hard to explain unless I have more time, but...well, would you mind asking her if she'd be willing to talk to me? Is she even home?"

The brunette shook her head vigorously, her smile calming Ashleigh's tattered nerves. "I'll be right back. Just wait right here," she said before scurrying away, partially closing the door.

Ashleigh waited five tension-filled minutes before the door was fully opened by a woman that appeared to be approximately Mona's age. Her hands, gnarled with age, clutched the door in barely suppressed rage. Her eyes were narrowed into slits of fury as she gazed at Ashleigh with disgust. "You want to talk to me about Elise *Cavendall*?" she spit, barely able to finish the sentence. "I can hardly couple her name with Cavendall! She was never fit to be a Cavendall! What do you want?" she demanded, her voice rising as her face blackened like a storm cloud.

Every instinct compelled Ashleigh to stand her ground. She stared directly into the piercing eyes of the woman before her. "So, you *are* a relative of Rodney and Elise Cavendall?"

"Of Rodney! Elise was nothing to this family! Why are you here?" she spat.

"I'm here because a dear friend of mine is dying, and she has a relative who had some connection to Elise. We're trying to understand that connection before my friend dies," Ashleigh asserted boldly, unflinchingly holding the woman's furious gaze.

"Don't you try this with me!" Elizabeth shouted. "Are you a member of Elise's family trying to pull a trick on me? After all these years? How dare you!" she screamed, nearly out of control. "Do you think that just because we couldn't prove what happened means we don't *know* what happened? Do you think we're *fools*? Get off my property *now*! And you tell the rest of them to leave us alone! Let us have our peace! Haven't they done enough already?" she shouted before slamming the door with a force that seemed to rock the entire house.

Ashleigh stared at the closed door in complete shock. She turned slowly and walked away, her legs barely supporting her as she got into her car and drove away. To where, she had no idea.

CHAPTER TWENTY

After leaving Winthrop Street, Ashleigh drove for thirty minutes before she felt confident enough to pull into a convenience store parking lot. She'd checked her rearview mirror continually after leaving the Cavendall home, fully expecting to see the flashing lights of a police car tailing her. The vision of being pulled over and questioned for trespassing on the Cavendall property kept her foot firmly glued to the gas pedal as she made her way out of Augusta.

Pulling into a parking spot at a Quick Stop Market, she turned off the ignition and rested her head on the steering wheel as pent-up sobs burst forth without restraint. She felt dirty and somehow tainted by the encounter with Elizabeth Cavendall. The secrets, the lies, the filthiness, the sin – a term she'd never been comfortable using at any point in her life until this moment – overwhelmed her.

After ten minutes, her cries retreated into quiet tears as she groped for the feeling of cleanness she'd experienced while reading the Gideon Bible in her hotel room the night before. So much of what she'd read seemed obscure and confusing, but amazingly, certain passages now stood out with startling clarity in her troubled mind.

As the cutting words of Elizabeth Cavendall returned, the language of Isaiah came back just as clearly. *Your lips have spoken falsehood, your tongue mutters wickedness.* Despite her sincere desire to help Mona, the futility of the search and the constant dead ends caused her to question why the truth seemed to elude her. *But your iniquities have made a separation*

between you and your God, and your sins have
hidden His face from you, so that he does not hear.

Was it possible that God was blocking her
path to the truth? Stopping her in her tracks
each step of the way? Had her sins created a
chasm so wide that God didn't hear her
desperate prayers on Mona's behalf?

A passage she'd practically memorized by
reading it repeatedly seemed to audibly call out
to her as customers went in and out of the Quick
Stop Market, oblivious to her personal turmoil.
Seek the Lord while He may be found; Call upon Him
while He is near. Let the wicked forsake his way, And
the unrighteous man his thoughts; And let him
return to the Lord, And He will have compassion on
him; And to our God, For He will abundantly
pardon.

Ashleigh shook her head in frustration as
she wiped the tears from beneath her eyes. She
couldn't make sense of her own thoughts or
what to do next. She wanted to hear Stephen's

voice. To be reassured by his certainty that she would somehow find the answers Mona needed. *But what is Stephen's certainty in light of God's determination?* she reasoned. If what she'd read was true, it was God alone who held the outcome in his hands. No matter how confident she or Stephen might be that it would all work out the way they wanted it to.

The thought of Stephen took Ashleigh down another avenue of confusion as she sat in the parking lot. She could no longer ignore the ache in her heart every time she talked to him or thought about him. Her mind lingered on the moment she'd seen him transform before her eyes from cold and untouchable to warm and vulnerable.

She would never forget him standing before his mother's grave and the instantaneous revelation of the man he truly was. The man he'd kept carefully hidden behind a wall of self-preservation. She realized that it could take years to get to know some people, but for others it took only a single moment of elucidation to see their soul. With Stephen, that moment had come, but she was left now with confusion and uncertainty.

She had repressed her feelings for Stephen since that night, the words from his own lips confirming that he would never be able to cross the chasm of the past to freely love someone. *I vowed that day never to give myself to anyone the way she did. There's an instability that consumes a person when they love that deeply.* It seemed a lifetime ago since Stephen had uttered those two sentences which cut off any hope she'd begun to feel when she first saw him at his mother's graveside.

As she considered the pain it would cost her to love him from a distance, she felt as if her heart was being ripped in two. Yet, she knew she loved him. She knew she would always love him. And she knew there was no choice but to love him from afar rather than not at all. Love never offered any options to the heart. It was a self-burning fire that couldn't be extinguished.

One of the teens loitering on the sidewalk suddenly hit the hood of her car, causing Ashleigh to jump and scream as her thoughts were abruptly interrupted by the loud noise. The group of older kids erupted into squeals of laughter when she started the car and backed up. She quickly headed for the exit and onto the Interstate.

Driving along the highway in quiet solitude, she found her thoughts drifting back to what had transpired at the Cavendall home. As she struggled to make sense of it, she wondered what Elizabeth Cavendall's words could have meant. *Do you think that just because we couldn't* **prove** *what happened means we don't* **know** *what happened?*

The insinuation following that spiteful question was that Elise's family had somehow been involved in whatever it was that had so wounded the Cavendall's, igniting Elizabeth Cavendall's rage. The end result was that more mystery now shrouded the search for Mona's peace.

Ashleigh reached across to the passenger seat and grabbed her phone. She glanced down intermittently, dialing the nursing home's number. It was now or never. A friendly woman named Dalia answered, connecting her with Mona. It took nearly ten rings before Ashleigh heard Mona's raspy and weary voice on the other end.

She cringed at the sound, filled with dread as she became even more aware that Mona's days on earth were dwindling away. She wished she was at Rose Manor to comfort Mona instead of heading who-knows-where down a dark interstate. "Mona, it's me," she said softly.

"It's so good to hear your voice!" Mona

exclaimed.

"It's good to hear yours, too. I miss you."

"And I miss you…terribly," Mona responded.

"I hear Stephen has been taking good care of you, though," Ashleigh said, her heart aching as she mentioned his name.

There was a long pause before Mona answered. "Ashleigh, I know that neither one of us thought much of Stephen in the past, but…"

"But what?" Ashleigh asked, holding her breath.

"I don't think he's what we thought he was. I'm afraid we misjudged him. He's a wonderful man. Just afraid, I think, of showing who he is deep down inside."

"I think you're right, Mona," Ashleigh said hoarsely, the ache in her heart now an open wound.

Mona sensed that Ashleigh was struggling, and she intuitively guessed why.

She quickly changed the subject. "What news do you have for me?"

Ashleigh took a deep breath, steeling herself for what lie ahead. "I found a relative of Rodney's today...Elizabeth Cavendall," she offered, putting off the moment when she would have to break the news about Sophie.

"Oh, my! What did she say about Rodney and Elise?" Mona asked eagerly.

"I barely got two words out before she went after me. She was *very* angry," Ashleigh said, recalling the hatred in the woman's eyes. "The Cavendall family apparently despised both Elise and her family. It seems they blame Elise's family for something horrible that happened, although I didn't get enough time with Elizabeth Cavendall to fully understand what she was implying. She kicked me off her property before I had time to ask any questions."

Ashleigh heard Mona's sharp intake of breath after she had relayed the information.

"There's more. I also found a monument in Kittery today. It was erected in Elise's memory...by someone who obviously loved her very much."

"Stephen told me about the monument for Elise this afternoon after he talked to you...and that there's no monument for Rodney. Do you think it could have been my father who put up the monument for Elise?"

"It's a very real possibility based on the letter from Elise to your father. If so, that would explain one of the spots on his map...and she died in Ogunquit...that covers another point that was marked. Saco is the only town that seems to have no apparent connection to the map...at least not one that I've been able to uncover yet."

"And you haven't found anything in regard to Eunice, or anything that ties Eunice and Elise together?" Mona asked, her tone tinged with desperation.

Ashleigh winced. "Mona, I'm afraid I

have some difficult news I need to share with you. I don't want either of us to jump to conclusions about what it means, but…please brace yourself as I explain this to you. Do you remember mentioning to Stephen that you felt Eunice's face may have been burned?"

"Yes, of course."

"Well…" Ashleigh began and haltingly proceeded to detail everything she'd learned from the private investigator in regard to Sophie's conviction for attempted arson in 1916 and her subsequent release in 1917. "It doesn't mean that that Eunice and your mother's attempted arson conviction are in any way related…it's just…I had to tell you. I knew you would want to know." As Ashleigh's words trailed into silence, Mona was completely silent. "Mona, are you okay? Please talk to me! I'm so sorry, Mona!"

"What else do you need to tell me?" she heard Mona ask quietly.

"How did you know?" Ashleigh asked, her heart breaking for Mona.

"You don't live as long as I have without being able to sense reservation in a person's voice. Just tell me," Mona said weakly.

In obedience to her wish, Mona revealed the conversation Peter had overheard between Mona's parents when he was a young boy – as well as his interpretation of what it meant.

"He thought I might have been adopted?" Mona asked incredulously.

"Yes, but your birth certificate disproves that."

"But you said my birth certificate was never filed with the city of Canton. That they have no official record of me being born there, correct?"

"Yes," Ashleigh sighed.

"More lies...more lies," Mona cried. "Everywhere we turn. Lie after lie."

"Mona, I'm *so sorry*," Ashleigh

floundered, desperately trying to soothe her.

For a full minute, Mona didn't respond. Ashleigh could hear her labored breathing and the occasional sniff that revealed Mona was softly crying. For reasons she couldn't fully understand, she felt compelled to remain silent as Mona sifted through the deceit surrounding her life.

Finally, Mona spoke. "Here's what I want you to do next," she said decisively. "I want you to go to Gouverneur, New York. Eunice and Elise can wait. I know my mother didn't start that fire, Ashleigh. And you're going to Gouverneur to prove it."

CHAPTER TWENTY-ONE

Ashleigh peeled her legs from the seat of the metal folding chair in the sweltering storage room, gazing hopelessly at the mountain of case files surrounding her as she stood up to stretch. "Of all days for the air conditioning to be on the fritz," she muttered to herself, tucking a rebellious strand of blonde hair into the knot at the nape of her neck.

She'd been searching for Sophie's case file for three hours and had yet to find even one scrap of paper that detailed the facts regarding her attempted arson conviction. "And what else did I expect? It happened *ninety* years ago," she said out loud.

As she muttered the words, the door to

the storage room slowly creaked open. The thirty-something police sergeant, Tom Samson, popped his head in. Ashleigh smiled at him warmly. Earlier that morning, he'd graciously listened to her heartfelt plea to research the closed case files and had helped Ashleigh get started on her hunt by directing her to the storage room where all the old files were stored. In New York City she probably would have been laughed out of the police station, but Gouverneur, New York was a slice of small-town America that still greeted visitors with welcome rather than skepticism.

"How's it going?" he asked, smiling cheerfully.

"Oh *great*," Ashleigh responded sarcastically, pointing to the myriad of files littering the floor and sticking haphazardly out of several file cabinets. "If you're the type of person who enjoys the looking-for-a-needle-in-a-haystack brand of torture."

Tom laughed and walked into the room, a fan in his right hand. "I thought you could use this," he said, kneeling to plug the dilapidated machine into an outlet in the wall. His brown eyes danced as the sudden gust of air emitted a grateful sigh from Ashleigh.

"Thank you so much! I was just about to die in here."

Tom stood up, nonchalantly tucking his hands into his pockets. "I'm on lunch now if you'd like an assistant," he offered, smiling again.

Ashleigh paused uncertainly. She was thankful for his willingness to help, but she'd gathered from his periodic visits to the storage room throughout the morning that he was interested in getting to know her better. She'd sensed from the moment she met Tom earlier in the day that he was a great guy. The kind of person that was rarely troubled by anything, sweet and completely uncomplicated. The exact opposite of Stephen.

Tom was looking at her curiously, waiting for a response. "Sorry," Ashleigh smiled apologetically. "I was lost in thought. Sure, it would be wonderful to have some help."

"Okay, then!" he replied energetically as Ashleigh sat down. Tom folded his six-foot frame into a tight spot between two stacks of folders on the floor across from her. Sweat was already beginning to bead beneath the strands of blonde hair that fell casually onto his forehead. "Remind me of the name you're looking for?" he asked.

"When the arrest occurred, her name was Sophia Ross. She was arrested and convicted of attempted arson in 1916."

Tom whistled. "Wow, that's a long time ago. Are you able to tell me more about why this is so important?" he asked curiously.

Ashleigh looked at the floor, unsure if she had the emotional energy to begin another account of Mona's past and the present search for answers. But Tom had been so accommodating that Ashleigh felt obligated to offer him some explanation for her investigation. "It's an incredibly long story. I'm a nurse at a nursing home in Ohio."

"Ohio?" Tom interrupted, his face registering disappointment.

"Yes," Ashleigh said, hopeful that mentioning she lived out of state would put an end to any interest Tom might have in her. "Anyway, a patient of mine is dying and something happened in her past that she desperately needs answers about before she dies. I'm trying, although not very successfully, to help her find those answers. Finding the file for Sophia Ross could help me better understand a piece of the puzzle about my patient's past."

Tom stared at Ashleigh, making no attempt to hide his admiration. "That's absolutely wonderful."

"Well, I love her..." Ashleigh said, blushing as she picked up a tattered file from the floor and leafed through its contents. Sensing Ashleigh's reservation, Tom followed her lead by picking up several files, determinedly probing through each one for the name Sophia Ross.

After ten minutes of silence, with multiple files discarded beside each of them, he cleared his throat, breaking the hushed stillness in the room. "No luck?" he asked good-naturedly.

"No luck. I assume you haven't had any either?" Ashleigh said dejectedly.

"Unfortunately, no...and it's about time for me to get back to work," he said, brushing his pants off as he stood up. "If you're still here after I'm through with my shift, I'd love to take you to dinner," he said quietly, his eyes sweeping her face for a reaction to his invitation.

Ashleigh took a deep breath as she held his gaze, his brown eyes full of the same cheerful warmth that had appealed to her when she first met him. "I'm sorry, Tom...I really appreciate the offer, but..."

"But there's someone else," he finished for her, his friendly grimace indicating this wasn't the first time he'd heard words like those.

"Well, in all honesty, there isn't anyone. At least not as far as an actual relationship...but there's someone in my heart. And to me, that's just as real as if there *was* a relationship. I've tried, but I can't ignore how I feel. Does that make any sense?" she asked, looking up at Tom with sincerity in her features.

"Yes, it *does* make sense. I've been there before, and I know what you're saying. I appreciate your honesty, Ashleigh." He paused, looking down at his hands and then back up at her. "But if you ever have a change of heart, don't forget old Tom Samson in Gouverneur," he chuckled good-humoredly.

"I won't," Ashleigh smiled warmly.

"Okay, then. Good luck with the search.
Let me know if you need anything."

"Thank you so much, Tom!" Ashleigh
called out. He glanced back before walking
through the doorway, nodding in
acknowledgment of her gratitude before
disappearing down the hall.

For the next two hours, Ashleigh sifted
through hundreds of torn and tattered records in
search of Sophie Krane's history, her frustration
growing with every passing minute. She was on
the verge of throwing a temper tantrum as the
warmth of the room and her fruitless search
stretched her patience to the breaking point.
Only the thought of Tom's reaction kept her
from dumping every single file on the floor and
screaming at the top of her lungs.

Her back and shoulders ached, her head
was throbbing, and the heat was oppressive.
Ashleigh experienced a wave of irrational anger
as she reached to the very back of a metal file

drawer and grabbed the next file, jerking it out and opening it defiantly.

Then suddenly, the words *Sophia Lee Ross* jumped out at her. Her throat seized shut as she read the words typed across the top of the page. She backed away from the cabinet, clutching the file in disbelief. She sat down, her hands shaking as her eyes sped over the document hungrily, poring over every point of the police report detailing the facts surrounding Sophie's arrest. The police had found Sophie at the home of Jason and Isabelle Davis at three in the morning, the side of the house completely doused with gasoline, a gas can in Sophie's hand, and matches in the pocket of her dress.

Ashleigh tore through witness reports, reading the statement from the local grocer who claimed that Sophie had bought a large box of matches at his store just the day before, as well as white cotton cloths and various grocery items. An employee at the local hardware store had signed a statement in which he outlined Sophie's purchase of a container of gasoline two days before the crime had occurred. The arresting officer had written a vivid description of Sophie's vehement assertion of her innocence despite all the evidence to the contrary. A motive was also supplied in a lengthy diatribe by the detective. Jason Davis and Sophie's father, Michael, had been involved in a bitter legal dispute before Michael and Gwyneth Ross had died in a buggy accident, supplying the motivation for Sophie's actions.

Ashleigh set the file down on her knees, trying to control her rising panic. It was her worst nightmare come true – the irrefutable facts of Sophie's guilt in black and white. *But if her guilt was obvious, why was she released only a year later*? Ashleigh wondered.

There was one page left in the file and she reached for it, her heart beating wildly. The arresting officer had written a closing script to the case a year later, indicating that Sophie had been granted an early release before the completion of her four-year prison sentence.

A final paragraph stated that the judge who had overseen Sophie's conviction had made a final ruling in her case ordering that all pertinent details leading to the cause of her release were to remain sealed. *"Noooo!"* Ashleigh moaned as she slammed the file shut and threw it violently across the room.

CHAPTER TWENTY-TWO

Exhausted, Ashleigh walked out of the Gouverneur police station thirty minutes later after making copies of Sophie's entire file and saying a friendly good-bye to Tom. She looked both ways before stepping off the curb and heading across the street to where her rental was parked.

Halfway across the road she stopped abruptly, frozen in shock. Leaning casually against his car was Stephen, a wide smile lighting his face. He shrugged his shoulders as he pulled his hands from the pockets of his faded Levi's. His deep blue eyes shone with happiness, and Ashleigh knew in a moment of truth that it was because of her.

"What...what..." she stammered, her eyes locked with his, her heart pounding so hard she could feel it throbbing in her ears. She knew no matter what happened between them in the future, she would never forget how he looked at this moment – relaxed, unbelievably handsome, mischievous, and tender.

Stephen laughed, motioning her forward. "Come on! Hurry up! I know this is small-town America, but if you keep standing in the middle of the road, you're going to get hit."

With legs that felt like rubber, Ashleigh approached him slowly, his expression growing less playful and more serious as she drew closer. As she stood beside him, they stared at one another, both searching for what they hoped to find in the other's heart. Confirmation came for Stephen in the hesitant smile and the shimmering tears in Ashleigh's eyes – hers in the sober intensity of the emotion that filled his.

"I don't understand," Ashleigh

whispered as the tears brimming in her eyes dropped onto her cheeks.

"I don't know that I entirely understand, either. I had a feeling this trip to Gouverneur wouldn't turn out well, and I wanted to be with you. I didn't want you to have to go through it alone," Stephen said softly.

"Why?" Ashleigh asked, barely able to form the word.

Stephen sighed heavily, his eyes darting toward the street and then back to Ashleigh. Hope, fear, and anticipation all played across his features as he moved a step closer to Ashleigh and reached for her hands, taking them gently in his own. Stunned and ecstatic, she returned his grasp with warm reassurance.

"I'm not going to play games with you. I'm afraid. I don't want to hurt you, but I'm terrified I will. I have so much pain and anger bottled up inside of me." He shook his head, frustrated with his inability to express all he wanted to say. "Ashleigh, I love you. I think I've loved you for a long time. I love everything about you...your compassion, your sense of humor, your intelligence...everything. I need you to teach me to love again. I want that, yet I'm so afraid of it. I need you to help me get to the point where I know it's okay if I can't erase the pain that will inevitably come into your life...and to be certain that if I can't take it away, I won't lose you like I lost my mom."

He searched her face earnestly, his raw emotion engulfing them both in a tide of never-before experienced feelings. "Can we take it one day at a time and see what happens? Can we try? Do I even stand a chance with you? Could you ever love me?"

"*Ever* began that night in the cemetery when I saw the real Stephen. I love you...I love *you*."

Relief and joy flooded Stephen's face as he took her in his arms, cradling her head against his chest as they cried together, the unknown journey into the future having begun for them both.

***

They sat in a secluded corner of the restaurant, the light from the candles flickering on their faces. "So, what are you going to do next?" Stephen asked softly as they waited for their dinner. The beautiful melody created by the pianist at the baby grand piano filled the room, easing them through the newness of being alone together.

Ashleigh was conflicted, struggling to keep her mind focused on the importance of finding answers for Mona, yet overwhelmed by the fact that Stephen was actually sitting across from her, and that he loved her. "I don't know. When I feel like I'm starting to get a grip on part of the puzzle, I run into a dead-end. It's almost as if...well...I don't know..."

"What? What were you going to say?"

Ashleigh looked down, fidgeting with the napkin in her lap. "Well...I've been so upset and confused by everything that's happened...so, the other night at the hotel, I read a Bible that was in my room. I was searching for something. Answers...I don't know."

She stopped, looking up at Stephen, uncertain of his reaction. He smiled tenderly, giving her the courage to continue. "I started reading this section called Isaiah. It said that God is the one who determines the end from the beginning. That all people are sinners...that our sin causes a separation between us and God. So much so, He can't hear our prayers unless we turn to Him. After reading that, I've wondered repeatedly if God is preventing me from finding the truth. If he even hears my pleas that Mona would be given some peace before she dies...if He's blocking my way until I turn to Him. For the first time in my life, I've experienced the sensation that I *am* sinful. I don't know," she said, fumbling for words, "Does that make any sense? Do you think I'm crazy?" she asked, embarrassed and confused.

"I've thought about the reality of God so many times since my mom died. But mostly along the lines of 'if there's really a God, how could He have let this happen?'" he admitted, fingering his silverware distractedly.

"But what if the things that happen to us are for a purpose far bigger than we can comprehend or see?" Ashleigh questioned. "I read another verse that said, *My thoughts are higher than your thoughts and My ways higher than your ways.* It made me wonder if we can truly see things clearly that we're not viewing from God's perspective. If what I read is true, that is," she finished. As she did, a picture of Stephen finding his mom after she'd taken her life leapt to her mind, and her cheeks burned with shame.

"Please don't think that my thinking out loud about this means I'm trying to minimize the pain you've experienced after what happened with your mom! Please don't think I'm doing that!"

Stephen reached across the table, and she offered her hand, joining it with his. "Ashleigh, if there's anything I know about you, it's that you would never intentionally cause anyone pain. I wish I could believe in God. If there's a bigger picture, I hope I'll be able to see it someday. Right now…I can't see it," he said truthfully, gently squeezing her fingers.

The waitress appeared at that moment, speaking melodramatically as she set their plates in front of them with a warning that they would be hot. Ashleigh caught the twinkle in Stephen's eye as the waitress voiced her desire for them to have a wonderful dinner and swished away with all the faux-Hollywood glamour she could muster.

They burst into subdued laughter when

the coast was clear. "What was *that*?" Stephen chuckled.

"I have *no* idea," Ashleigh laughed.

"Yeesh, scary," Stephen grimaced as he picked up his knife and fork, diving into the steak the waitress had just set before him.

Ashleigh's heart was full as she sliced into the grilled chicken on her plate, feeling truly happy for the first time in weeks. An elation she'd never experienced before gave her joyful hope about the future.

Completely wrapped up in the moment, she was startled when her phone suddenly began ringing. She grabbed her purse from the floor and dug through it, quickly pushing the mute button. As she gazed down at the name on the caller ID, all the color drained from her face.

"What? What's the matter?" Stephen asked. "Is it someone from work?"

"No, it's *Elizabeth Cavendall*," she said, stupefied.

"Hurry, answer it!" Stephen urged, leaning forward in eager anticipation.

Ashleigh hit the talk button, trying with all her might to sound confident. "Hello?"

"Who *are you*?" Elizabeth Cavendall asked haughtily.

"Who are *you*?" Ashleigh retorted, her courage rising to meet Elizabeth Cavendall's bristling arrogance.

"You know full well who I am! I'm certain you have caller ID on your phone. This is Elizabeth Cavendall, and you know it."

"And I'm certain you know who I am, or you wouldn't have been able to reach me on my cell phone," Ashleigh countered defiantly. Leaning forward, Stephen nodded his head in approval of Ashleigh's strong rebuttal.

"Oh, I know who you are. The Cavendall's have enough money to obtain information on most anyone. What I want to know is what are you up to?"

"If you were so interested in knowing, why did you slam the door in my face?"

"Young lady *do not* get smart with me," Elizabeth hissed threateningly. "What are you up to?"

"I tried to tell you what I was *up to*," Ashleigh responded, barely able to restrain her temper. "A friend of mine has a relative who had some connection to Elise in the past, and we're trying to understand that connection."

"Well, isn't that the vaguest sentence I've ever heard uttered," Elizabeth raged. "Now, I want you to listen to me very carefully. If anyone in that family tries to taint the Cavendall name like they did in 1919, I *swear* to you, you will *pay* for it! Remember that, Miss Ashleigh Craig. It's the furthest thing from an idle threat you'll ever receive," Elizabeth Cavendall said menacingly before the line went dead.

CHAPTER TWENTY-THREE

"What did she say?" Stephen pressed as Ashleigh laid her phone on the table with trembling hands. She'd talked a good talk with Elizabeth Cavendall, but she was shaken up. She described the brief conversation to Stephen in detail, her face clouded with bewilderment the entire time.

"She's the one being intentionally vague. I bet she doesn't know who you are other than your name. She obviously doesn't want to tell you *how* the Cavendall name was tainted by Elise's family. She isn't saying a lot because she isn't sure how much you know. During both conversations you had with her, she never mentioned Elise's maiden name. I think she hasn't mentioned it because she doesn't want you to know it…just in case you aren't already familiar with it. She's afraid if you don't already know Elise's maiden name and she gives it to you, then you might seek them out and talk to them. That's my opinion. She's nervous, but smart."

Ashleigh looked at him in amazement. "And I don't know *anything*! I wish I did!"

"But Elizabeth Cavendall doesn't know that. She's most definitely covering her tracks. I wonder what happened in 1919 to cause such hatred between the families that Elizabeth is still very angry about it."

"I think she's about the same age as Mona. She would have been a young child in 1919. Whatever happened, it must have affected her family to such a horrible degree that she still carries that grudge even after all this time. What could it have been?" Ashleigh questioned, finally picking up her fork and taking a bite of the chicken.

"When you talked to Elizabeth Cavendall at her home, she implied that Elise's family had done something terribly wrong. Something the Cavendall's knew they'd done but couldn't prove. Then she calls you worried that Elise's family is trying to taint the *Cavendall* name. So, that means Elise's family must have accused the Cavendall's of something at some point in the past. But the two different statements just don't fit together. It doesn't make sense."

Stephen paused, fingering his fork, his steak still untouched. "Rodney and Elizabeth Cavendall died in 1919. Maybe it was something in regard to their deaths. Maybe Elise's family tried to blame the Cavendall's for what happened to them. But that doesn't work either," Stephen said, shaking his head. "The Cavendall's despised Elise for some reason, but they apparently adored Rodney...the Cavendall's having anything to do with his death doesn't seem plausible."

"And the way things are going in this so-called investigation of mine, we'll probably *never* know," Ashleigh said, discouragement creeping into her voice.

Stephen took her hand again, smiling gently. The warmth in his eyes took Ashleigh's breath away. "You know what? You need some time off. No more talking about Elizabeth Cavendall. Let's enjoy our dinner then go down to the river."

Ashleigh smiled in return, the realization of how much she loved him dawning anew. He had asked her to teach him to love again, but Ashleigh had the definite impression that *he* would be the one to teach *her* what it truly meant to love.

***

Ninety minutes later found them on a

scenic outlook overlooking the St. Lawrence River, their fingers intertwined, reveling in everything as if they were seeing it for the first time. The stars, the moon and love itself seemed as new as if they had been born that day.

"I was wondering about your family. What are they like?" Stephen asked, watching the dark ripples of the water cresting in the moonlight.

"My family, huh? Are you sure you want to know?" Ashleigh laughed.

"I *think*?" Stephen joked, picking up on her playful mood.

"Well, let's see...I have just one sister who is four years younger than me. Her name is Tracy...and other than the fact that she's the star in the soap opera she calls life, she's pretty normal. My dad's name is Matthew and he's a wonderful guy. A giant teddy bear...but very protective of his little girls," Ashleigh said slyly, teasing Stephen. "And my mom's name is

Susan. She's my best friend. I couldn't ask for a better mom. She actually came to your defense once," Ashleigh said, getting Stephen's immediate attention.

"How so?" he asked, surprised.

"I spent the afternoon with my mom after you issued my written warning and gave me the day off to think about what a bad girl I'd been."

Stephen winced. "I know you're kidding, but I was wrong about that, Ashleigh. Just so wrong. Being unkind was my way of keeping you at arms-length. I was trying to kill my feelings for you." The soft breeze whipped gently at Ashleigh's waist-length blonde hair as Stephen watched her in the moonlight, his heart aching to be completely free of the fear that had kept him from her for so long. "So, tell me how your mom defended me."

"She told me that I needed to look beyond the surface. That I should delve a little deeper. That you may have experienced some pain in your life that was causing you to act the way you were," Ashleigh sighed, regret lingering in her words.

"I think I'm going to like your mom very much," Stephen laughed, ribbing her with his elbow as they leaned on the metal railing of the overlook. Drinking in the magical aura of the evening, they watched the river in silence, afraid that uttering a sound would break the spell of the night. The subtle smell of the pine woods below wafted upward, filling their senses.

"Are you thinking about your mom?" she asked, stroking Stephen's hand.

"I am. I was wishing she could have known you."

Ashleigh swallowed back tears as she watched Stephen's profile in the moonlit darkness, memorizing every line of the face that was now so beloved. "I wish I could have known her, too."

"I found a poem by her body the day she

died," he said so softly Ashleigh could barely hear him.

"What did it say?" she asked gently, sensing that he wanted to share it with her.

A distant look masked his face as he quietly recited the poem, its words enveloping him in its cadence of hopelessness.

"Love comes swiftly

Yet its death dawns slowly

So foolish to think the gift would be given

Even to the lowly

If I am hidden from you

That's the way you want it to be

If I turn and show you my pain

Look for once – let yourself see

You will run

Afraid of the real me

Why do you accuse when I laugh

Instead of crying

Why do you point your finger when I smile

Instead of sighing

You didn't care that I was an illusion
In keeping with your lie
So why would your heart break
If my spirit were to die?"

Bitter tears stung Ashleigh's eyes as she turned to Stephen and took him in her arms, holding him with all the strength within her. The pain seemed to erupt from an unfathomable pit deep within him as he began to sob.

The voiceless cries which had been hidden for years were now wrenched from the very center of his being and given full expression. He drew from Ashleigh's strength, clinging to her like a child as he buried his face deep in her hair as the torrent burst forth. After ten minutes, the deluge subsided, and she stroked his hair soothingly as they held each other in the darkness.

"Stephen, she was in profound pain," Ashleigh whispered, her voice hushed in the stillness as the smooth-flowing river gurgled below.

"I know…but why didn't she try harder? Why didn't she love me enough to stay?" he asked, the long-buried question finally spoken aloud.

Ashleigh drew back, holding Stephen's face in her hands as she tenderly caressed away his tears. "It wasn't about whether she loved you enough to stay. Your mom's whole life was about loving you. You told me that. From the moment you were born, you were her life. There's no doubt about her love for you. Taking her own life wasn't about not loving you. She chose to end her life because of *her* pain…her own hopelessness. It wasn't about not loving you enough to stay. It was about *her*."

Stephen stared at Ashleigh as comprehension gradually emerged. "You're right. I've spent all these years making it about me. Blaming her…but all those things were about me. I was never really thinking about *her*.

I don't think she was weak, Ashleigh, I think she was tired."

"Too tired to go on...and you need to forgive her for that. She loved you, Stephen, but she'd fought for everything her whole life. There's no one to blame. Death as a release is never the answer, but sometimes people just can't see that when they're completely exhausted by pain."

"Please don't ever let me forget that," he said, his eyes loving her as he took in every detail of her face.

His cell phone suddenly rang, slicing through the moment like a machete. "What is it with us and being interrupted by phone calls?" he asked, pulling it from his pocket and looking down at the caller ID. "It's the nursing home," he said, glancing up at Ashleigh with trepidation. "Hello?" he answered quickly. For almost a minute he listened intently as the frail voice on the other end spoke softly. "Alright.

Okay, Mona. We'll be back as soon as possible," he said before pushing the end button.

"What? What is it?" Ashleigh questioned, her voice rising in panic.

Dumbfounded, Stephen stared at the phone in his hand, then at Ashleigh. "Mona said to come home. She said the search is over. She's been talking to Connie. She said she's already found her peace...*in Jesus Christ.*"

CHAPTER TWENTY-FOUR

Stephen and Ashleigh walked briskly down the hallway, anxious to get to Mona. Because of her failing health, she'd been moved out of the assisted living section of the nursing home and into a nursing unit where she could be continually monitored for any complications.

When they reached Mona's room, Ashleigh glanced anxiously at Stephen. Despite what Mona had said to Stephen on the phone the day before, she couldn't get past the feeling that she had failed the greatest task of her life by not uncovering the ghosts of September 5, 1926 – a day that would now haunt her just as it had haunted Mona. Stephen read her thoughts and gently squeezed her hand, letting her know without words that he was there to support her.

As he pushed the door open, Ashleigh entered the room quietly, Stephen following behind her. The room was dark except for the shred of evening light that peeked beneath the shade that had been pulled down to block the light. The air conditioner's muted hum buzzed in the background as Ashleigh's eyes rested on Mona's sleeping figure lying completely still in the hospital bed at the center of the room. Her heart swelled with terror as the thought that they were too late gripped her, but Mona's eyes fluttered at just that moment, relieving her anxiety.

Stephen took her hand, and they made their way across the room to Mona's bedside. Gazing down at Mona, Ashleigh was totally unprepared for what she saw. The same Mona she had known and loved for three years was there, yet somehow, she had been completely transformed. Ashleigh was in awe of the peace and light that seemed to radiate from Mona even as she slept. The deeply creased face exuded a new joy that Mona had never before possessed. Ashleigh looked over at Stephen, and his expression mirrored exactly the confusion and wonder in Ashleigh's own heart.

Mona's eyes fluttered again and then fully opened, a beautiful smile brightening her wrinkled face as she looked up at Ashleigh and Stephen. "Ahhh, you're finally here," she exclaimed, stretching her trembling hand toward Ashleigh's.

As their hands joined, Ashleigh bent down and kissed Mona's cheek. The weeks of pent-up frustration and failure finally found release as a flood of tears coursed down her face. "Mona, I'm so sorry! I tried. I tried so hard! Please forgive me. I..."

"Hush, child! Sweet Ashleigh...don't say such things. It will be alright. Sit down. I want to talk to you both."

Obediently, Stephen and Ashleigh took a seat in the chairs at Mona's bedside while she gazed at them with unabashed delight. "It's so *wonderful* to see you both again! My only regret now is that I sent you away, Ashleigh. I wasted precious moments I could have shared with you."

"Mona, I don't understand," Ashleigh said, holding the frail hands in her own. "What happened?"

Mona's eyes twinkled like the young girl of seven she'd been before Eunice had appeared at her home so long ago. "Connie came to visit the day before Stephen left for Gouverneur. She began to talk to me about Jesus...begging me to listen. Begging me to understand that I was on the verge of eternity. I knew she was sincere. For reasons I can't fully understand, I agreed to let her read the Bible to me...to explain her faith."

Mona paused, struggling for the breath to

continue. "She read to me about the life of Jesus...who the Bible says He is...God himself. We talked about passages that spoke of the reality of sin...of *my* sin...and that death exists because of sin. She talked to me about Christ and how He willingly went to the cross to bear the punishment for the sins of his people. He did it *willingly!* Can you believe that? Willingly! She told me about the joy and forgiveness she was granted when her eyes were finally opened, and she repented of her sin. It was so much to take in...and yet...I began to *see it*."

A rattling cough suddenly seized Mona, and Ashleigh hurriedly grabbed a glass of water off the bedside tray, holding it up to her lips so she could take several sips. As the attack subsided, Mona smiled weakly, her eyes alight with happiness. "I know I'm going to die, but I'm so *happy*. Connie read me a verse that I memorized very quickly," she said proudly. "*For God, who said, Light shall shine out of darkness, is the One who has shone in our hearts to give the light of the knowledge of the glory of God in the face of Christ.* I believed in Christ that day. I can't explain it, but I *know* that God shone light out of darkness and changed me. I once despised anything to do with God…and now you could never convince me that He's not real."

Ashleigh wiped tears from beneath her eyes as Mona took deep breaths, struggling desperately for the air to sustain her life. Ashleigh glanced at Stephen, his stricken expression breaking her heart.

"Stephen, please look at me," Mona said quietly. Stephen hesitantly turned his gaze to Mona, his eyes tormented with naked grief as he recalled the events of his troubled life. "I know your type of pain. I've lived with that kind of pain, too. I would still like to have answers to my questions about why certain things happened, but I know that God will reveal those things to me shortly. Stephen, there's no other road to peace. There will be no other answer for you other than the one that lies with Christ. Don't run from Him as long as I did. Learn from an old woman who is dying," she pleaded, her piercing appeal echoing eloquently in the quiet room.

Stephen looked away, unable to bear the searching intensity of Mona's eyes. Ashleigh reached for his hand and gripped it tightly, wishing she could infuse all the love she felt for him through her fingertips into his.

"Ashleigh," Mona whispered softly.

"Yes?" Ashleigh answered, refocusing her attention on Mona.

"I would like to ask you just one more favor. My mother had a Bible that she read nearly every day. In the past, I could never bear to look at it. After she died, I packed it away with all of her other things. I would love to have it now…just to hold it in my hands and read from it in the time that I have left. Knowing that her hands once held it, and that she read the same words, would be such a comfort to me. It's in a box at Connie's house along with many of my other things that are stored there. Would you mind going to Connie's and getting it for me? She'll know which box it's in."

"Of course! I'd do anything for you, you know that. I'll go right now!"

***

Connie opened the door to her small ranch home in an older allotment on the outskirts of North Canton, her face cheerfully pleasant as she invited Ashleigh in. "Hi, Ashleigh! It's so nice to see you again!"

"It's nice to see you again, too," Ashleigh said truthfully as she stepped into the house. The small home was comfortable and homey with photos perched on the piano in the corner of the living room, innumerable books lining shelves at the far end of the room, and half-finished cross stitch patterns scattered about. Connie was watching Ashleigh closely, her face beaming.

"I know why you're so happy today," Ashleigh said with a smile, graciously offering the carrot she knew Connie wanted.

"I'm ecstatic beyond words! It's a joy I can't even begin to describe!"

"I'm not going to pretend I understand what that means, Connie, but I'm happy for you." Ashleigh paused, uncertain as to whether she wanted to continue the conversation. The emotional intensity of the last several days and the confusion in her own mind regarding the things Mona had said to her and Stephen an hour earlier had the effect of making her want to retreat into a protective shell of silence.

To her own surprise, though, the words haltingly began tumbling out before she could stop them. "I read some of the Bible while I was away…verses in the book of Isaiah. I have so many questions. Parts of what I read were so beautiful and inspiring, and other things were so difficult to understand," Ashleigh said, fidgeting with her purse.

"I know," Connie said empathetically. "I experienced that same feeling when I began reading the Bible. It's normal. When we read the Bible, we find God there, and the depths of God are very deep, Ashleigh."

Connie's home phone abruptly began ringing, its shrill tones reverberating loudly throughout the house. She looked in the direction of the kitchen hesitantly, not wanting to lose the thread of conversation she and Ashleigh had begun.

Ashleigh noticed her hesitation. "Go ahead and answer it. I'll wait for you," she offered.

"Okay, thanks. There's the box you'll want setting there by the couch. Go ahead and look through it."

Ashleigh sat down on the blue and white gingham couch, making herself comfortable. She looked at the small box setting at her feet then reached for it, pulling it onto her lap. She carefully peeled away the packing tape and opened the corners, peering inside.

She saw the Bible right away, a large volume encased with a brown leather cover. She carefully lifted it out, placing the box on the floor again. She sighed as she looked at the worn leather casing, knowing that Sophie Krane's own hands had once touched it. Hands that ninety years ago had nearly set fire to a home with two innocent people sleeping inside. Ashleigh opened the cover and thumbed through the pages until she came to the book of Isaiah. As she did, the corner of a bulky sheaf of papers slipped out near the back of the Bible.

Her brows furrowed in curiosity as she carefully opened the Bible to the section where the pages had been placed. She removed the bundle of yellowed papers that were covered by a noticeably male script. Her heart began to beat furiously as she carefully opened the papers, noticing the date *August 10, 1971* at the very top of the page and the words *My beloved Sophie* beneath the date. It was a letter.

With shaking hands, Ashleigh flipped the letter over. The signature at the bottom caused her to cry out as if she'd been struck. The letter had been signed, *Forever Yours, Richard*. With instantaneous understanding, Ashleigh understood that God had now chosen to reveal what he had kept hidden from her until this moment. The answer had been there all along. *In Sophie Krane's Bible.*

Ashleigh flipped back to the beginning of the letter, reading its contents as if possessed, her mind numb with shock as the tragic secrets of Richard Krane's hidden life unfolded before her eyes. The words that exposed him and the consequences that had followed him to his grave seared her soul like the imprint of a branding iron.

When she'd finished the letter, she tried to call out to Connie, but her voice failed, and she sat mute in horror and grief. With violently trembling hands, she laid the letter on the pages of the Bible as her gaze fell with stunning clarity on the verse directly above her fingertips. *For nothing is hidden that will not be revealed, Nor is anything secret that will not be made known and come to light.*

CHAPTER TWENTY-FIVE

Ashleigh, Stephen, and Connie sat together at Mona's bedside, waiting as the nurse adjusted her oxygen. When the nurse was done, she smiled at the three somber faces before quietly leaving the room.

"So, you've found my answers after all?" Mona asked, surrounded by a halo of white hair as her head rested against the pillow. Rasping breaths came low and shallow in the dim room as the small light above the bed cast an angelic glow on her frail figure. She clasped her hands on her chest, her expression peaceful and resigned.

Ashleigh could only nod as she held Richard's letter in her shaking hands. Connie reached over, stroking Ashleigh's back soothingly.

"Please, read it. I'll be fine, Ashleigh. Whatever it says, I'm at peace with God. Nothing can take that from me. Nothing else *matters*," she said, her response resolute.

"Al…alright," Ashleigh faltered, barely able to speak. She opened the letter, glancing at Stephen for reassurance. The love reflected in his eyes gave her the strength she needed. Slowly, hesitantly, then with gathering courage, she read Richard Krane's words. The explanation Mona had waited a lifetime to hear.

August 10, 1971

My Beloved Sophie,

I've instructed my lawyer to give you this letter upon my death. By the time you read it, I will already be gone. I don't want to leave you. I don't want to die. I'm afraid. But then, I've always been a coward – as you'll clearly see by the close of this letter. In death, as I did in life, I will run from the consequences of my actions. Death will be my final and ultimate hiding place.

Sophie, I love you. I cannot say that enough. The contents of this letter will shock and hurt you. I only pray they don't destroy you. Please forgive me for what you are about to read. My only hope is that having loved me for so long, you will know my heart and forgive me for a lifetime of deceit.

I'm a dying man – and a dying man who needs to confess and make things right. Even now, I don't have the courage to face the two people I have wronged – you and Mona. I'm so ashamed. Too ashamed to see the betrayal in your and Mona's eyes. I despise my weakness, but I'm imprisoned by it. You don't know how many times through the years I would watch you while you slept, wanting to tell you everything. But I was too afraid. I didn't want to lose you, and I was so afraid I would if I told you the truth.

Sophie, how did this happen to me? How did I make such a disaster of this life that was given to me? I started into adulthood with such high hopes for the man I wanted to be, but the reality became something far different than the hopes.

For you to fully understand the motivation for what I did, I have to start at the beginning. Please be patient with me as I tell you about my childhood and my early adulthood. As you're aware, my mother died when I was nine. My father was an evil man. Something you're also aware of from the little you witnessed of his life before he died. What you don't know is that he was a murderer. He killed my mother. With one action? No. Slowly. Agonizingly. Silently. Year after year until he finally stripped her of her very soul. He beat her mercilessly. Day after day, week after week, until nothing remained but a cringing, terrified shell of a human being. Have you even seen a grown woman cower before a man like a dog, wetting her pants in fear? Have you ever seen a man laugh like he'd just heard a good joke while he kicked a woman in the face with every ounce of strength he possessed? Have you ever witnessed a man step on a woman's hand, crushing her bones as if he were merely squashing a spider? I have. I saw it all. Helpless to save my mother, I saw it all.

After she died, my father decided it was my turn to suffer. Almost the moment after she was placed in the ground, he began to beat me just as viciously as he'd tortured my mother. Tell me Sophie, what do we say about a society that turns its back on its most vulnerable members? For years, people turned their eyes away from the brutality imprinted on my face and body. Teachers who were afraid to help.

Others who weren't willing to involve themselves in such a sordid business as child abuse. Neighbors who felt it was none of their business as a helpless child was forced to drink from the pool of his own blood. Tell me, what excuse do we offer that could justify such inaction from these people? These participants in premeditated murder – just as surely as if they'd lifted their own fists to deliver the death blow?

By the time I was fifteen, I'd been beaten more times than I could count. My spirit was nearly broken. I'd thought of running away just as many times as I'd been attacked, but such is the irony of a person who has been abused – their death is imminent and yet they're afraid to leave the horrible normalcy they've always known. It's because of the manipulation of the abuser that those who are abused don't have a normal thought process. Their reasoning is shattered. Their minds malfunction because of the abuse.

Somehow, even after all of the beatings, a tiny remnant of personhood remained in me. Just a whisper, but enough to save me. The final straw came at last. As punishment for opening my father's grocery store one minute late, he locked me in the basement without food in the spring of 1911. During those days, he would set a bucket of toilet water on the first step of the basement stairs and tell me to drink it. Then he would laugh and slam the door shut, locking it behind him. Even though I could barely function from hunger, I was grateful that I hadn't been beaten. But every time the door opened, I wondered if my life was going to end that day.

Three days in, I discovered several boxes of my mother's books that had been thrown in the basement after her death. I found a favorite of hers – a pictorial volume about the state of Maine. One that I'd seen her look at time and time again with an expression of longing so

intense I could almost see her standing on its
beaches facing the vast ocean, the wind blowing
in her hair. Free at last from all pain. In the
back of the book, there was a map of the state.
As I read the book and learned about the history
of Maine, I developed a plan to run away and
see for my mother what she'd always dreamt of
seeing. If I could only make it out of the
basement alive.

I read about three towns on the southern
coast of Maine where it might be possible for me
to find work – Ogunquit, Saco and Kittery. The
town of Ogunquit was well-known for its
fishing trade, Saco for its industry, and Kittery
for its famous ship yard. I imagined it would be
possible to find some type of job in one of those
towns. Enough to rent a room and put food in
my stomach. I circled those three spots on the
map as a tangible way to keep me focused on my
goal of escape.

On night seven, I finally gathered what

little remained of my courage, painstakingly breaking out one of the basement windows piece by piece after several hours of silence from the upstairs. I desperately prayed that my father was asleep and that I was still small enough to squeeze out of the small basement window. I took the map of Maine but left the book behind.

After what seemed like hours, I finally made it out of the basement that night. My back was mangled and bloody from trying to fit through the window, but the beatings I'd endured at the hands of my father had more than prepared me for the pain. After freeing myself from the window frame, I never looked back. Despite the fact that I had a permanent limp as the result of my father smashing a cement block on my knee when I was eleven, I ran like the wind – and kept running until ten the next morning.

I know I told you when I first met you that my injury was the result of a work

accident. *After everything that happened –
which will unfold as you read this letter – I
couldn't tell you all that I'm telling you now. I
pray you can forgive me! Forgive me for all that
I've done to mislead you. At this point, I know
you don't understand. I need to keep writing.*

*After running all night long, I made it to
Akron. I asked directions and found the nearest
train station. With nothing but the clothes on
my back and a hidden dollar in my pocket, I
made my way east, finally arriving in Maine a
month later. How I got there with so many odds
against me was a miracle. A miracle that
restored my faith in humanity. Person after
person took pity on me, giving me food, shelter,
or an extra dollar. Complete strangers without
whose help I would be dead today. I wonder if
the haunted look in my eyes compelled them to
have mercy on me. I will never know, nor will I
ever forget what they did to save my life in the
spring of 1911.*

After arriving in Ogunquit, I met a kind fisherman named John Dorman. For two years, I boarded with him, his wife Lily, and their young daughter Frances, learning the trade and saving what money I earned. They were beautiful people, and as John taught me the trade of fishing, he taught me the lessons of life as well. I found in him the fatherly love I'd never known before. It was because of him that I consciously began to evaluate the type of man I wanted to be, and I purposefully set about to emulate John's strength, tenderness, wisdom, and insatiable love of learning.

When I was seventeen, he died of a sudden and massive heart attack. His death was a blow that affected me almost as deeply as my mother's. For a year afterward, I cared for Lily and Frances to the best of my ability, but when Lily remarried, I decided to go to Kittery to try my hand at working in the shipyard. I had fallen in love with the ocean from the time I first set foot on Ogunquit's white beaches and felt there would be nothing better I could do than to craft the vessels that faced both the ocean's wrath and serenity on a daily basis.

I'd saved a good amount of money during my time with the Dorman's, and after saying good-bye, I left with my suitcase in hand on May 1, 1914 and traveled to Kittery. I rented a room atop a local tavern and immediately applied for a job at the shipyard. I was hired the day I applied. For three years, I toiled to learn the craft of shipbuilding by day, advancing steadily to the position of foreman. By night, I frequented the library, voraciously reading everything I could get my hands on in an effort to grow into John's Dorman's likeness.

It was June 9, 1917, in the library at Kittery that I met Elise Patterson – the young woman who altered the course of my entire life.

CHAPTER TWENTY-SIX

Sophie, please forgive me. Please don't hate me for never telling you about Elise. I've never told you about any of what you're about to read. Please know as you read this that I love you more than I ever dreamed it was possible to love another person. You're the anchor of my heart. You have been my reason for going on all these years. Without your love, I would have been lost. Please remember that as I try to explain.

As I said, I met Elise Patterson at the library in Kittery, Maine in 1917. I was twenty-one years old. Elise was nineteen. She came in that evening and sat at a table near mine. She had a stack of books a mile high and went right to work on her studies, never even noticing me. I was instantly enchanted by her. I could tell by watching her throughout the evening that she was desperate to learn. Almost as if it were a matter of life and death. As if she was trying to escape a prison of ignorance that had kept her shackled and bound. I was to learn later that what I'd guessed was true.

After several hours, Elise fell asleep over her books. I watched her sleep for twenty minutes before finding the courage to walk over to her. I knew the library would be closing within minutes, so I gently woke her up. She was embarrassed, but grateful for my kindness. That moment of introduction was the first in a series of moments that Elise and I spent together that summer, and we fell deeply in love. The consequences of that love affect me even to this day and will follow me into the depths of my grave.

I discovered while walking Elise to her

employer's home that evening that she had come to Kittery because of her job. She was from Augusta but had traveled to the coast in her service as a nanny for the Cavendall's. They were a wealthy family she worked for, and they were vacationing in Kittery for the summer. From the moment Elise and I began to talk, there was a common bond of suffering and pain that drove us together and gave us understanding of one another's hearts.

Elise had been born into extreme poverty. She was the oldest of ten children. Her father died of tuberculosis when she was fifteen, leaving Elise's mom a widow and his ten children fatherless. Elise had worked to help the family since the time she was a young girl, but there was never enough money. She and her family were always near the point of starvation with barely enough clothes to cover their backs. While the rest of Augusta seemed to thrive around them, they lived in its slums, caught in a trap of horrific poverty.

As the summer passed, I could sense a growing tension in Elise. It finally came to a head near the end of the summer when I asked her to marry me on the beach at Kittery as the sun rose on August 22, 1917. I'll never forget her tears as she explained to me that the Cavendall's eldest son, Rodney, had proposed to her before the family left for Kittery in late May. When she hesitated to accept, he asked her to consider his offer of marriage over the summer. Rodney had stayed behind to manage the family business while his parents and younger brothers and sisters vacationed. He was twenty-five and heir apparent to the family fortune, and as such, filled the place of his father in managing the company whenever Morris Cavendall was away.

Elise explained to me that Rodney's family knew nothing of his love for her and that because she was a penniless no one, with nothing to offer that would raise the Cavendall status higher in society, there would be unimaginable opposition if she were to accept Rodney's proposal. I couldn't believe what I was hearing. I demanded to know if she loved him. I can't forget that scene on the beach that morning as the sun rose into the sky. Elise clung to me in tears, telling me how much she loved me. She said she didn't love Rodney despite what a wonderful man he was. A man whose character stood in complete contrast to the arrogance and cruelty of the rest of his family. I knew as I held her in my arms that there was a 'but' coming.

She begged me to understand her indecision. She explained that marrying Rodney would give her the ability to free her family from a future of abject poverty. Elise knew the ability to release them was in her hands. If she said yes to Rodney's proposal, her mother and her siblings would live out the remainder of their lives without any worries. If she said no, she would watch them all suffer, knowing she had chosen selfishness over self-denial. It was something that had tormented her that summer as we fell deeper in love. Her heart was breaking, yet I had nothing to offer but my love. I was uneducated in the formal sense of the word and just a foreman of a shipbuilding crew. I could clearly see my future and expected to live modestly for the rest of my life. I couldn't give Elise what Rodney Cavendall offered her.

Elise and the Cavendall's left Kittery a week later, but she continued to write over the next four months, having asked Rodney to wait on her answer, torn between her love for me and her duty to her family. I wish I could say Rodney was a bad man, but he wasn't. He was exactly the opposite. I wish I could have hated Elise for her indecision. But life isn't always black and white.

Finally, in December of 1917, I received

the letter that sealed my fate. President Wilson
had declared war on Germany on April 6, 1917,
and despite the vehement objections of his
family, Rodney Cavendall enlisted. He begged
Elise to marry him before he was sent to Europe.
First bound by duty and now bound by honor,
the final decision was made. Elise agreed to
marry Rodney Cavendall. It was a bitter
moment for me in so many ways. Rodney had
enlisted, unintentionally evoking Elise's
sympathy, and I could not even be drafted due to
my limp.

I wrote to Elise pleading with her to
reconsider, giving every scenario I could think of
to convince her that we could find a way to
provide for her family. The only answer I
received was a short note saying she understood
how difficult it was for me to understand her
decision. Telling me that she would always love
me and asking me to keep her in my heart
forever. Elise and Rodney were married on

January 5, 1918. Yes, I know you're very familiar with this date. I will explain. Please, bear with me. Rodney was deployed to Europe shortly thereafter. Sometime after Rodney's deployment, I learned from Sarah Stolins, a friend Elise had made during her summer in Kittery, that Elise was pregnant. I'd thought of her almost every second since the time she'd left, but if possible, I thought of her more then. Wondering how she was and what she felt as she carried the child of a man who might never return from the battlefields of Europe.

There was nothing left for me to do at that point. I continued on with my life, but there was a void in me I was certain would never be filled. I took the high school equivalency exam, passed it and finally entered a night program at the local college. I had a desperate desire to advance myself in the world, and probably subconsciously, I was trying to find a way to better myself to make it possible for me to provide for Elise's family if Rodney never made it home.

The months passed and as the war wound to a close in November of 1918, I learned from Sarah that Elise had given birth that month to a beautiful dark-haired baby girl named Patricia Anne Cavendall. Rodney survived the war and returned home late in December of 1918. He had fought valiantly and was awarded the Medal of Honor for showing conspicuous courage above and beyond the call of duty during the Second Battle of Marne in July of 1918. I'm sure it was a proud moment for him and Elise.

Again, the months passed as I continued to work toward my degree at the local college, my heart still raw. In late May of 1919, Sarah came to me again, telling me that there would be a celebration in Ogunquit in June in honor of the men from the state of Maine who'd fought during the war – and that Rodney and Elise would be present at the ceremonies so that

Rodney could be recognized for receiving the Medal of Honor. I fought a terrible internal battle that week, but I finally succumbed to the desire to see Elise just once more. I traveled to Ogunquit for the celebrations the first weekend in June of 1919.

I was careful to move with the crowds those few days on that Friday and Saturday, knowing that I would cause Elise pain by my presence there if she were to see me. I watched her from afar, so proud despite my pain. Proud of the selflessness she'd chosen, proud of the courageous woman she'd become. Along with a group of other people, I snapped a picture of her and Rodney while they posed on Ogunquit's beautiful white beach – the strong Medal of Honor recipient and his beautiful wife. It was the last picture of Rodney and Elise Cavendall that was ever to be taken.

That Sunday morning, Elise and Rodney were specially invited by the mayor of Ogunquit to take a day-long pleasure cruise on his boat. I stayed in Ogunquit that Sunday as many others did. They enjoyed the food and festivities, but I was just waiting for a final glimpse of Elise. As the day came to a close, I heard the news that I would never see Elise again. Sometime during their day at sea, the mayor's boat had capsized. Although the search continued along the coast for a week, none of their bodies were ever found. I knew for certain from the summer I spent with Elise in Kittery that she didn't know how to swim. She was probably lost to the sea within minutes. I imagine that Mayor Jenkins and Rodney died trying to save her.

To describe the depth of my pain during that time is useless. I wandered the shores of Ogunquit's beaches for a week, overwhelmed with more sorrow than I thought a soul could humanly endure. I'm not telling you about my feelings then to hurt you, my dear and precious Sophie! I'm only telling you how I felt so you can clearly understand what drove me to do the things I later did. You have had my entire heart through our years together! You have been my everything!

After the loss of Elise, I returned to Kittery. I commissioned a monument to be erected in her memory, and in the ground beneath it, buried all her letters to me – except for the final note she'd sent me. That note, and the photograph I took of Rodney and Elise on Ogunquit beach, are the only things I kept to remember her by.

As I sat by that monument day after day, I had the idea to set up an anonymous trust for Elise's daughter, Patricia. In my mind, it would be a tangible way to pay tribute to the memory of the woman I'd loved. I learned from the newspaper that Rodney's family was going to raise Patricia, and that she was already living with them in the well-to-do area of Winthrop Street in Augusta.

On September 30, 1919, I left for Augusta to set up the anonymous trust for Patricia Anne Cavendall in memory of Elise. That fateful trip haunts me to this very day.

CHAPTER TWENTY-SEVEN

By the time the bank closed the following day, I had succeeded in setting up the trust for Patricia at a local bank in Augusta with all paths to me untraceable. I used an alias to set up the account, giving specific instructions that the name on the trust was never to be revealed. In this day and age, it seems remarkable that such a thing could be done, but as you know, 1919 was a completely different era.

After leaving the bank, I was suddenly consumed by a desire to see Elise's child. The only connection to her that remained in the world. I asked a local where I could find the Cavendall home, and he easily directed me to their house on Winthrop Street. I arrived at the

Cavendall home around five, walking casually along the sidewalks, hoping I would somehow be able to catch a glimpse of Elise's ten-month-old daughter. What I heard and saw next caused me to make a decision that changed not only my life, but the lives of so many people.

From a first-floor window of the Cavendall's home that was opened to the street, I heard a child screaming. I knew that scream as well as I knew the bloody lines on my father's fist. It was the scream of a child being abused. Looking around and seeing no one, I hid among the shrubbery lining the Cavendall property, and made my way along the side of the house to a large window that was open.

As I looked in, I saw a young twenty-something woman slap the beautiful dark-haired child that was sitting on the sofa. I knew without a doubt that it was Patricia – she was a perfect miniature of Elise. I'll never forget the words that spewed from that woman's mouth.

"You little brat! You threw up on my outfit! We have somewhere to be in ten minutes! I hate you! No one in this house wants you! You're only here because we couldn't let a child with the name Cavendall be raised by those filthy Patterson's!" As Patricia continued to cry, the woman grew more agitated, shrieking at her to shut up. In the next moment, Patricia vomited again. She was clearly ill. The woman started screaming at the top of her lungs. She was insane, Sophie. She was my father all over again – only in female form.

I watched in horror as she scooped up the vomit, pushing it back into Patricia's mouth. It made her gag and caused her to vomit again. "That will teach you to make me late, you little brat!" She was clenching her teeth and her face was contorted with rage. It was as if I'd been struck by the lightning of my past as I stood looking through that window, unnoticed. The force of it paralyzed me. I couldn't move.

A few seconds later, a servant rushed into the room and grabbed Patricia off of the sofa. She said, "Miss June, you go now. I'll take Miss Patricia for you. Little Miss Elizabeth is all dressed and ready. You just go on. We'll be fine." I watched as the woman – who I later learned was Rodney's sister-in-law, June – stare at Patricia with utter hatred. You could tell she was barely able to control her rage, wanting more than anything to hit her. The poor servant stood there nearly frightened to death.

June finally stormed from the room and the servant sank to the sofa the second she left, cradling Patricia and soothing her cries. "What's to become of you, Miss Patricia? You don't deserve this. Miss June is an evil, wicked woman. Poor baby, what is to become of you? Your poor Mama never done anything like Miss June does to you. Never!" The servant calmed Patricia and rocked her to sleep, eventually carrying her upstairs.

In a moment, all the brutality at the hands of my father rushed back to my mind. I had witnessed the same cruelty in June Cavendall's eyes that I'd seen in my father's eyes countless times. I could have answered that servant's question. I knew what Patricia's life would be like. I could see her future as plainly as if it were already a reality. I saw Elise's baby at ten, cowering before June Cavendall as she kicked her in the teeth, laughing while the blood dripped at her feet.

Elise's face suddenly appeared before my eyes, begging me to save her baby. I knew in a single second what I was going to do. I knew the Patterson's stood no earthly hope of gaining custody of Patricia even if I did report what I'd seen to the police. In a world where the Cavendall's had the money to pull all the strings, the Patterson's would be completely disregarded. If Patricia was to be saved, I was the only one who could do it.

How I pulled it off, I'll never know. I hid in the thick shrubbery for hours, my resolve growing rather than weakening. My love for Elise silenced any doubts that crept into my mind. During those long hours, I was energized by a passion to see justice done to people like my father and June Cavendall. I was filled with a need for revenge. It was unlike anything I'd experienced even during the years of my father's vicious cruelty.

I waited several hours after every sound had faded and every light in the house had gone out. Then I walked to the back of the house and tried the servant's entrance. As I'd expected of those who presume they live in complete safety, it was unlocked. I made my way through the kitchen into the spacious first floor of the house, then climbed the staircase to the second floor. Every creak of the steps, every whisper of the wind through the windows was a nightmare of hellish proportions, but I wasn't afraid for myself. I was terrified that I wouldn't be able to save Patricia – that Elise's haunted face would torture me for the rest of my life. Minutes later, I was able to locate the nursery.

As I stood over the crib looking down at Elise mirrored in the image of Patricia's tiny face, I knew there was no turning back. Patricia smiled up at me in the moonlight, calming every fear. It was as if she trusted me completely the moment that she set eyes on me. As if she had been given some divine revelation that I was to be her salvation. I reached into the crib, and she held her arms out to me as I scooped her into mine. I grabbed a coat and several changes of clothes from the armoire in the nursery and shoved them into a cloth sack that I found in the armoire. Miraculously, Patricia never cried as we left the Cavendall home. She was quiet the entire night as we fled to safety.

I made it back to Kittery just before dawn, whisking Patricia into the room I rented above the tavern before anyone was awake. Exhausted, yet too terrified to sleep, I formulated a plan while Patricia finally dozed off, contentedly resting in the center of my bed. As I brushed the dark ringlets away from her face, I cried as I'd never cried, releasing all the years of pain at my father's hands – and crying out to Elise – begging her to guide me now that the fate of her child rested solely in my hands.

The next day was a blur. I had to leave Patricia alone briefly while she was sleeping. I was terrified to leave her, but I had no choice. I went to the bank in Kittery and withdrew all my savings. I told my landlord that I needed to leave to help my dying mother. It was a lie, but no one ever thought twice about questioning the quiet, sad loner who lived above the tavern. I was nearly sick with relief when I opened the door to my room to find Patricia still resting quietly. I waited until the patrons in the tavern got loud and rowdy, then fled in the darkness, hiding Patricia in my coat as I left my room. I put her in a small basket beside me in my Model-T and covered her with blankets.

I could feel Elise's presence protecting us as we made our way out of Maine, heading toward a land I prayed would forever conceal us. The rolling green hills of a place I'd only read about. A place where I felt it would be safe to hide, presenting myself as a widower with an infant daughter. I planned to hide among the quiet, unsuspicious Mennonites of Lancaster, Pennsylvania. It was there that Patricia Anne Cavendall became Mona Joy Krane. Please forgive me for lying! Please forgive me for telling you that I was a widower who'd lost his wife in childbirth. I never wanted to deceive you, but I was so afraid of the Cavendall's finding me!

I lived in constant fear of being discovered those first few weeks as I settled into my two-room home in Lancaster. I found a job working as a clerk at Miller's Hardware – a fact of which you are very much aware. The place where we first met. With all the experience I'd gained at my father's grocery, the job suited me perfectly. I was constantly looking over my shoulder. I watched the newspapers for stories about Rodney and Elise Cavendall's missing child. I started to breathe easier as the days passed. The headlines confirmed that I'd been successful in escaping Augusta unnoticed. There were absolutely no witnesses to my coming and going from the Cavendall home, and instead of searching for an outside intruder, the recriminations and accusations were flying between the Cavendall's and Elise's family. The Cavendall's accused the Patterson's of abducting and hiding Patricia in an unknown location, and the Patterson's accused the Cavendall's of abusing and possibly killing Patricia.

The servants were interviewed by the

authorities, the abuse was confirmed, and though the police investigated, they couldn't find any evidence of foul play. The peers of the Cavendall's whispered amongst themselves about the possibility that June Cavendall could be responsible for Patricia's murder. From that day on, June and Michael Cavendall, and their daughter, Elizabeth, were spurned by the social circle of the wealthy and powerful in Augusta. A fitting and deserved justice for June Cavendall.

I took no joy from the accounts I read, but the words gave me hope that Elise's child could live out her days in happiness and security. Though June Cavendall's abuse had been confirmed through the investigation following Patricia's (Mona's) disappearance, there was no way I could return Mona. I knew the law would show no mercy to a heartsick man who'd been compelled by his past to rescue a child from a similar fate. I was certain I would be arrested and imprisoned. In addition to that, I feared that the Cavendall's would somehow be able to pay off a judge and reestablish custody. If Patricia was given to Elise's mother, she would more than likely collapse under the strain of having another child to feed. There was no option but to continue in the course I'd chosen when I decided to save her.

And then, Sophie, I found you. You have been the embodiment of every dream I'd ever had for a loving wife. If only that dream hadn't included the nightmare of Eunice – how different our lives would have been.

CHAPTER TWENTY-EIGHT

The moment you walked into Miller's Hardware, I had the strangest feeling I'd found my true home. I'll never forget the way you carried yourself. With the quiet dignity of a person who had truly suffered. And your eyes. Eyes that were filled with sympathy and kindness – eyes that I love to this very day. After Elise died, I thought I'd never love again, and I fought my feelings for you at first, thinking to care for someone so soon after her death was disloyalty to her. But as our love grew from friendship over the next several months, I knew it was time to break with the past and move forward with the life with you that I longed for.

As we took long walks that winter and you told me about your past, I wanted to tell you about Mona and what I'd done in taking her from the Cavendall's but fear always stopped me. By then I'd fallen in love with you, and I didn't want to lose you. As you unfolded the story of your past, I despised Eunice for what she'd done to you. It amazed me that you were so free of bitterness. How many people could have gone through what you had and not been eaten alive by anger? How many people could have lost a year of their lives as the result of protecting an aunt who was mentally ill and not desire revenge? Your pity for Eunice made me love you even more.

As you told me about your Aunt Eunice and the schizophrenia that had eaten away at her mind, and the love your parents had shown in caring for her rather than committing her to a mental asylum, I marveled that such self-denial existed in the world. When you spoke so softly *about how you'd held Eunice in your arms as a young teenager, covering her face with cold cloths after she tried to set fire to your parent's home, succeeding only in burning her own arms and face, I was so ashamed of my shallowness. Even after your mother and father died and you were forced to care for Eunice alone, you displayed a depth of character I only dream of possessing.*

Why couldn't I have shown the courage you did the night you discovered Eunice trying to set fire to Jason and Isabelle Davis' home? Why didn't I have the strength you had after you realized she'd escaped from the house and you tracked her down and took the matches from her and fought her for the gas can, sacrificing yourself to the police after Eunice ran and hid? I didn't even come close to doing those kinds of thing when my freedom was threatened. I despise myself, and I'm so afraid you will hate me when you know what I've done. I realize none of what I'm saying makes sense to you right now. I'm trying to tell you, but the shame is unbearable. I'll try to finish.

As we walked the hills of Lancaster that winter, and you told me how Eunice's mysterious disappearance a year after your attempted arson conviction finally made it possible for you to go to the judge with your claim of innocence, I wanted so badly to confess the truth about Mona to you. Thank God the judge believed your claims and ordered your release after reading your parent's journals detailing Eunice's illness. That he sealed the records in order to protect himself from disbarment made me realize how much he'd risked saving you from more time in prison. He knew you stood no chance in a second trial with the circumstantial evidence against you, and I'll be forever grateful to him for acting with courage. If he hadn't freed you when he did, I might never have met you in Lancaster.

Do you remember March 18, 1920, when I asked you to be my wife? It's a silly question. I know you remember. You'll recall how I asked you if you could agree to raise Mona believing that you were her biological mother – to raise her believing that we'd married on Rodney and Elise's wedding anniversary rather than the one that was to be ours. You agreed, not knowing then why that date was so relevant. Now you do. I was covering all my tracks, even with you. I know as Mona grew older, what you once agreed to so readily, you struggled with – especially after giving birth to Peter. You wanted Mona to know about her mother. To be able to honor the woman who'd given birth to her. And you wanted to put an end to the deception.

Please forgive me for how harsh I was with you those times when you asked if we could tell Mona the truth regarding her biological mother. I was terrified. Terrified that *if you started asking questions and digging into Mona's past, my deceit would be laid bare. That all my lies would be revealed. That you would leave me. It was a chance I couldn't take.*

What you don't know is that Eunice did reappear – twice. You never had any knowledge of either of those events. You've lived the whole of your life thinking that because there had been no one to care for Eunice during your imprisonment, that she'd disappeared from Gouverneur, driven by her madness, and was probably roaming the streets somewhere. You've often said that she probably died completely alone and of some illness due to exposure or lack of care. Sophie, how do I even begin to tell you what truly happened to Eunice? God forgive me!

Eight months after our wedding, Eunice appeared at our home when you were away caring for Genevive Housman's children while she was ill. I knew who it was as soon as I opened the door. The leering sneer, the burn scars, the wild mass of dark hair – all those things told me it was your Aunt Eunice. She started screaming, telling me that friends you still corresponded with in Gouverneur had told her that you'd moved to Lancaster, Pennsylvania, and married a man named Richard Krane. She terrified me, Sophie. She was demented with rage, saying you'd abandoned her. If possible, I loved you even more in that moment. To know that you'd sacrificed yourself for the crazed animal that stood before me was more than I could ever imagine doing.

I invited her into the house against my better judgment, but I knew you would want to see her. Mona woke up from her nap as Eunice sat down at the kitchen table, voraciously tearing into a sandwich I'd left lying there. I excused myself to get Mona, wishing you were there to help me. When I brought Mona into the room, Eunice stopped eating, and her eyes opened wie. Almost with a monstrous joy. She started giggling, then doubled over in a fit of laughter while pointing at Mona. She asked me, "What are you doing with that Cavendall baby? I've seen her pictures in the paper. I would know that baby anywhere!" She began laughing again, pounding her fists on the table in insane delight. And then suddenly she stopped the banging. I was paralyzed with fear. My face gave me away and Eunice knew she was right. As mad as she was, she was right.

She stood up and approached me, sticking her finger in my face. "You've been a very naughty boy, haven't you?" I'll never forget her eyes. They were filled with utter malice. I knew I had to do something, and quickly. As she went from room to room in the house, distracted by voices in her head, I phoned the police and told them that an intruder who was clearly insane had forced her way into our home. The paddy *wagon was there within fifteen minutes. They dragged her away, kicking and screaming and clawing at them like an animal. The police never even questioned my story, and I never told you about what happened that day. But I knew I was living on borrowed time. I knew we needed to escape, and the only place I could think to go at that moment was home – home to North Canton, Ohio.*

As you now know, I never fully revealed to you what happened during my childhood. After taking Mona, I didn't have the courage to reveal the abuse I'd suffered at the hands of my father, thinking that if you ever read about Patricia Cavendall, you would somehow put all the pieces together and I would be exposed. I was so afraid of losing you. I know I've said that repeatedly in this letter, but that was always my greatest fear. Even more than prison, I feared losing you and your love and respect. As I'm sure you'll remember, when you returned from Genevive's, I told you that I felt the need to return to my roots, to go home after having made my way in the world alone for so many years. That I wanted to raise Mona surrounded by family. Your parents were gone and to your knowledge, you no longer had Eunice to care for, so you agreed to go. Sophie, then and always you have loved me sacrificially. You always trusted my judgment. How often through the years I felt I'd rather die than disappoint you.

You know what happened next. We arrived in North Canton in February of 1921, and I faced my father for the first time since I was fifteen. When I first saw him, a frail man, broken by his own wickedness, I felt triumphant. I felt that I had risen victorious over his barbarism. I loved you and Mona, and I knew I was a good father and a loving husband who had never once considered raising his fists against a helpless woman or child. I had finally *won. I was the victor and my father the defeated – and he knew it. I asked each of my relatives to respect my privacy regarding the years I'd been gone. I told them that you and I and our child wanted to start anew with no questions asked. Through the years, they honored that request. They never brought up the past and acted as if we'd always been a part of their lives. I will never forget that kindness on the part of my Uncle Jacob and my cousin Daniel.*

After several weeks in North Canton, I looked up an old school friend named David Skinner and found that he was working in the administrative offices for the city of Canton. He knew what I'd suffered at the hands of my father and was only too happy to help me when I asked for his assistance with forging a birth certificate for Mona. I told him that I'd been widowed before marrying you and that I wanted Mona to grow up believing that you were her real mother – that it would be so much easier that way. The fact that you were aware of the false birth certificate and had agreed to it at the time, also soothed my conscience. It all seemed so easy. So very easy. Until Eunice appeared on our doorstep on September 5, 1926.

CHAPTER TWENTY-NINE

*It was the day that changed everything,
and you still have no knowledge of it. The day
Mona lost her father. The day the respect I'd
always gloried in began to recede from your
eyes. September 5, 1926 – a day that has stalked
me like a cold-blooded killer. I still don't know
how Eunice found out where we were living. I
will never know now. Maybe from your friends
in Gouverneur, maybe through purposefully
searching for us, but she showed up at our house
in 1926, and once again you were away.*

*I was reading while Mona was playing
on the floor by the fireplace, and Peter was
napping. I can see Mona so clearly as I lay here
dying. How she looked up at me with eyes full*

of adoration, and how I returned her gaze with a loving smile. She was the picture of Elise and had proven to be nothing but a joy and comfort all the years since I'd taken her from the Cavendall's. I had never once regretted the decision. My only regret was that I'd hidden her past from you. The smile I gave Mona at that moment before the knock at the door was the last smile she would ever receive from me.

I got up to answer the door, and I looked through the window before turning the doorknob. When I saw Eunice's face distorted by impatient rage, my blood ran cold. I felt hatred and terror all at the same time. I grabbed Mona and took her upstairs to her bedroom and told her to be completely quiet. Even now, Eunice's words echo in my ears. "I know you're in there, Richard! Open this door, or you'll regret it for the rest of your life! Open this door now!" Eunice kept knocking, and Peter woke up crying, probably frightened by the sound. When she heard Peter, Eunice began to scream even louder. "How dare you! How dare you think you could do that to me! Didn't you think I would find you?"

I knew I had no choice but to confront her and try to get rid of her before you got home. I told Mona again that she needed to be perfectly still, and that she should not open the door no matter what happened. I went down and tried to talk sense into Eunice, but the same crazed madness that I'd seen in her in 1920 was still there. She wouldn't listen to reason. She pushed her way into the house and began to run up the steps. I don't know what she was intending to do, but I knew I had to stop her. I yelled at her to stop as she rushed upstairs. When I got to the top of the steps, she began to attack me, clawing at my face and body. A few seconds later, Mona opened the door to her bedroom and ran out, screaming at Eunice to stop. Eunice froze and stared at Mona. The day at our home in

Lancaster seemed to return to her mind. She knew she was once again seeing Patricia Anne Cavendall. She threw back her head and laughed – the evillest laugh I've ever heard. I could plainly see that my life was about to be destroyed. That a woman driven mad by schizophrenia held my freedom and my very life in her grasp.

And then it happened. In the moment of decision, I became my father. I was filled with rage and a desire to silence her forever. I was transformed from a man to a beast. I reached for Eunice and shoved her down the steps with all my strength. I watched, satisfied, as her body careened down the steps and landed at the bottom of the staircase. As I looked down on her contorted body, I remember thinking that her dark hair was the perfect covering for the sneer that had been directed at me just moments earlier. But as I continued to stare at Eunice's body, I returned to my senses. I looked down at my hands – hands that had succumbed to brutality as a solution. At that moment, Mona ran up to me and hugged me as I stood there paralyzed. She didn't understand what had happened, but she was trying to comfort me.

At that moment I snapped. I was never again to be the man I'd once been. My spirit was broken. For some irrational reason, I blamed Mona for causing me to become just like my father. I convinced myself that if she hadn't come out of her room, I wouldn't have been driven to the point of violence with Eunice. Bitterness toward her took hold of me like poison. I thought of all that I'd sacrificed for Mona's well-being, and how she'd repaid me by forcing me to violence. The little girl I'd so dearly loved, I suddenly hated. I could barely stand to look at her. I screamed at her and blamed her for what I'd done to Eunice. She was terrified. I'll never forget the look in her eyes. The confusion, the betrayal, the sorrow.

Does a real man force a child to carry that kind of guilt? Does a real man break the heart of a little girl and turn a cold shoulder to the torment in her eyes? Now you know who you've been married to all these years. You deserved better. Mona deserved better. Now you understand why I call myself a coward. I carried that irrational hatred toward Mona within me for years. An honorable man would have held himself responsible for his own actions. I didn't. I blamed Mona instead. Do you see my disgusting weakness? My cowardice? The injustice of it all? Do you see what I am? I'm no better than my father – no better than June Cavendall! I'd prided myself on being a better human being than them, but I discovered that I'd been made in their image after all.

I'm exhausted, but I need to finish. I thought Eunice was dead, but while I was shouting at Mona, Eunice began to moan at the bottom of the steps. She was alive! It was my last chance to save myself. I grabbed Mona and locked her in Peter's bedroom. I told her to take care of him and not to leave his room until I returned. Fear was written all over her face, but I was unfeeling. I did nothing to comfort her. I left Peter and Mona and ran downstairs. Eunice was alive, but barely conscious. I picked her up and carried her to the garage and put her in the backseat of the car. I knew exactly where I needed to go – the Massillon State Mental Institution. By the time I pulled up to the entrance of Massillon State, Eunice was fully conscious and ready to fight. When I got her out of the car, she started clawing at me and spitting in my face. Two orderlies rushed from the building and pulled her off me. They asked me to wait in the lobby as they struggled to get her into a room at the end of the hall. A few minutes later, the director came out to talk to me. I told him that I didn't know who Eunice *was, that she'd started banging on my front door and had rushed into my house, attacking me and threatening my children.*

All the time I was talking to the director, I could hear Eunice screaming in the room at the end of the hall. The director shook his head. He said, "We see this all the time. We'll take care of it." Eunice's dirty, disheveled appearance and her obvious insanity compared to my clean-cut image worked to my advantage. No questions were asked, and I walked away. I left her there in that madhouse and I never saw her again. Through the years, I called periodically to check on her. From what I was told, her schizophrenia only grew worse, and she eventually became catatonic and finally passed away six years after she showed up at our door.

Now you know everything, Sophie. My confession is complete. What awaits a man like me after this life I leave in the hands of the Almighty. But I know what I deserve. Even hell would be too kind a judgment for me. Facing death has made me answer for what I did all those years ago – the thing that has caused me to truly release Mona from the blame that should have always been mine alone to carry. How confused and afraid she must have been by what happened with Eunice and by the change in my attitude toward her from that day forward – and by the unbreakable silence with which I sealed it. As I reflect on it now, I wonder – would it have been kinder to leave her with the Cavendall's after all?

Sophie, please tell Mona that I love her. Tell her that I've always loved her. I know in my heart that I loved her all along, but the dye was cast that horrible day, and I couldn't get past it to express my love for her. Why couldn't I change? Why did I condemn myself and Mona to a lifetime of pain? I wish so desperately that I could take it all back, but it's too late now. Please let her know how proud I was when she *played Annie Oakley in her high school play. She was a natural! Tell her how beautiful she looked on her wedding day, and how proud and utterly undeserving I felt to walk down the aisle with her on my arm. Kiss her for me. Beg her to forgive me! I'm too afraid to ask for her forgiveness myself. I'm afraid of what I'll see in her eyes – that she'll despise me even more than she already does. Even now, I'm a coward.*

I plead for only one mercy from God as I face eternity – that the vision of your face would never be erased from my mind. Sophie, my beloved angel, I love you. I love you more than I ever imagined it was possible to love someone. Forgive me, my angel! I beg you, forgive me!

Forever Yours,
Richard

CHAPTER THIRTY

The room was silent except for the sound of sobbing. Ashleigh laid her head beside Mona's face, clutching Richard's letter as they cried together in the dim light of the room. Mona reached for Ashleigh, caressing her hair with trembling hands. Connie slid into the chair next to Stephen, gripping his hand as cries were torn from deep within him.

"Mona! Oh, Mona! I'm so sorry. *I'm so sorry!*" Ashleigh wept, her voice muffled against Mona's shoulder.

"The shock must have killed her," Mona whispered as delicate teardrops streamed down her weary face.

"What do you mean?" Ashleigh asked as

she lifted her head, her gaze blurred with tears.

"Do you remember when I told you that my mother died two days after my father?" Ashleigh nodded silently in answer to Mona's question. "The lawyer must have brought the letter that day. I remember him coming to the door when I was at the house helping mother with funeral arrangements for father. She must have read the letter after I left and then put it in her Bible. The shock must have killed her."

As Ashleigh sat back down in the chair at her side, Mona took a deep breath and closed her eyes. When she opened them again, her expression was thoughtful. "Connie, do you remember those verses you read to me the other day...the verses about what we were before we repented and turned to Christ?" Mona asked.

"Yes, I do."

"Will you read them to me again, please?"

"Of course," Connie responded, reaching for Sophie's Bible laying on the nightstand beside Mona's bed. She quickly thumbed through the Bible, and finding the passage, read the words in a clear, strong voice. "For we also once were foolish ourselves, disobedient, deceived, enslaved to various lusts and pleasures, spending our life in malice and envy, hateful, hating one another. But when the kindness of God our Savior and His love for mankind appeared, He saved us, not on the basis of deeds which we have done in righteousness, but according to His mercy, by the washing of regeneration and renewing by the Holy Spirit, whom He poured out upon us richly through Jesus Christ our Savior."

As Connie finished reading, there was a pregnant silence in the room as all eyes focused on Mona. "Yes, that's it. You see, I'm no better than my father. I'm a sinner. He was a sinner. I won't condemn him for the mistakes he made. I just hope and pray that he made his peace with Jesus before he died. As for me, it's enough to know he loved me. *It's enough,*" she said, her luminous smile lighting the room with joy.

***

They stood before the mound of brown earth as the frigid October wind whipped at them. Stephen encircled Ashleigh in his arms as she buried her head in his chest. Everyone had left and only they remained. He pulled a tissue from his pocket, wiping her tears as she looked up at him. "It was a beautiful funeral, wasn't it?" she asked, her words heavy with grief.

"It was," he said tenderly, caressing away the remaining moisture beneath her eyes. Ashleigh laid her head against his chest again, staring at the ground which now housed Mona beneath its depths.

"What are you thinking right now?" she asked, wondering if Stephen was reliving the pain of his mother's death.

"Do you really want to know?"

"I really want to know," Ashleigh said, holding him tightly.

"I was thinking that I want you to be my wife. I was thinking that I don't want to waste another day being afraid. I love you so much. Please…love me back by spending the rest of your life with me. Marry me?" Stephen asked hesitantly, his voice breaking as she looked up at him in wonder, her brown eyes lost beneath a pool of joyous tears.

EPILOGUE

Ashleigh paused as she came to the end of The Marginal Way, watching them in the distance as they romped in the shallow water. Stephen playfully showered their eighteen-month-old twins with water to squeals of gleeful delight.

She smiled as she watched him swing fair, dark-haired Maggie into the air, bringing her down and holding her tightly against his chest the moment he realized she was afraid. Matthew, blonde and tan, yanked on his daddy's swimming trunks, begging for a turn.

Ashleigh reflected on the last time she'd stood on the white sands of Ogunquit beach – and the walk back when she'd thought of Stephen. As she watched him now, a man transformed by her love and his new-found faith in Jesus, she could hardly believe he was the same person.

They had married on December 24, 2006, two months after Mona's passing from death to life. Their journey to that same life hadn't been as flawless as Mona's. For months, they struggled with doubt, fear, and unbelief, until God decided it was time, pulling them from the pit of sin and shining the light of Christ into their darkness.

As Ashleigh walked across the white sand toward the three people she loved most in the world, she thought of Elise and Richard and the love lost off the shores of this paradise. She sighed as she pictured Sophie reading Richard's letter, and the pain that must have cut her like a knife. And lastly of Mona, and all the sorrow she had endured during her life. But as Mona herself had said, "It's enough to know he loved me. It's enough."

The twins, finally spotting their mom, ran toward her as fast as their toddler legs could carry them. "Mommy! Mommy!" they shouted as Stephen followed close behind, his blue eyes mischievous.

"Did you have a good nap?" he asked, wrapping tendrils of Ashleigh's hair around his fingers as he bent to kiss her. The twins pulled at Ashleigh's sundress, begging to be picked up. Stephen smiled, his lips resting against hers. "We're lucky, aren't we?" he murmured softly.

"You know better than that," she teasingly reprimanded. "Luck isn't a word we use any more. We're blessed. Blessed beyond measure."

"How right you are. As usual." He pulled her close, his lips finding hers once again as the twins gave up all hope of being held, deciding to build a sandcastle at their parents' feet instead.

Made in United States
North Haven, CT
29 September 2022

24686785R00232